EDDIE
AND THE JETS

BY JOHN ATTANAS

DARBY
CREEK
PUBLISHING

To my writing teacher, the late, great Isabelle Holland. I don't think she liked football, but she was a wonderful teacher.
—JA

Text copyright © 2005 by John Attanas
Cover copyright © 2005 by Darby Creek Publishing
Cover illustration by Terry Naughton

Cataloging-in-Publication

Attanas, John, 1962-
Eddie and the Jets : a novel / by John Attanas.
        p. ; cm.
ISBN-13: 978-1-58196-026-3
ISBN-10: 1-58196-026-3
Summary: Eddie Paulsen, sixth-grade football fanatic, is having the worst time of his life—his father moves out, his football team is not coming together, he likes his best friend's sister, and his friends think he's a jerk. Eddie and his father learn together what life's real priorities are.
1. Fathers and sons—Juvenile fiction. 2. Best friends—Juvenile fiction. 3. First loves—Juvenile fiction. 4. Football—Juvenile fiction. 5. Teamwork (Sports)—Juvenile fiction. [1. Fathers and sons—Fiction. 2. Best friends—Fiction. 3. First loves—Fiction. 4. Football—Fiction. 5. Teamwork (Sports)—Fiction.] I. Title.
PZ7.A866355 Ed 2005
[Fic] dc22
OCLC: 57190207

45456

Published by Darby Creek Publishing,
A division of Oxford Resources, Inc.
7858 Industrial Parkway
Plain City, OH 43064
www.darbycreekpublishing.com

Printed in the United States of America

2 4 6 8 10 9 7 5 3 1

1-58196-026-3

|CONTENTS|

Chapter One

FADE-OUT, FADE-IN...BOMB

My team, the Juniper Street Jets, was down, as usual, 28-7, to Kirby Carpenter's Giants when all of a sudden everything began to click.

First I threw a screen to Kenny Blatt, who scampered on his chicken-bone legs halfway toward a first down.

Then I threw a quick-out to big Mikey Mantello, who lumbered past Sammy Green and made the first down before Kirby tagged him.

Then I snapped one over the middle to Bobby Rodriguez, and he drove hard. We were almost at the goal line—or as the announcer on TV always says, "Knocking on the door."

Then we Jets huddled up.

"Okay. Kenny and Mikey. You guys go out left," I said, sucking in air and rubbing a glob of dirt off my nose. "Bobby, go for it all."

"All the way, Eddie?" Bobby asked, his dark eyes opening wide.

"Yeah," I said back. "A low down-and-out. Dive."

"Wow," he said, his eyes even wider.

I walked up to the line sure that we would get the touchdown. Kenny and Mikey didn't like the low down-and-out because they could get hurt running it. But Bobby loved the play because it was dangerous. He would do anything to catch a football, and the chance that he'd get bruised or scraped up never scared him off. Bobby understood sacrifice—all in the name of football.

I yelled, "Hike!" and grabbed the muddy football, dropping back to pass. As soon as I saw Bobby cut right, I threw the ball. Really low.

He dove for it, his long arms outstretched almost into the next county.

He slammed to the ground, the ball firmly in his hands.

"Yes!" I yelled.

"Wow," Bobby said, smiling up from the dirt.

We threw off to the Giants. They couldn't go anywhere and had to punt after three quick downs.

Right away, we started moving again.

I placed a pass to Kenny so perfectly that he caught it without having to move his hands.

I tossed a lateral to Mikey, who scooped it like a bowling ball in his big hands and rumbled for a first down.

I fired another, just over Sammy Green's outstretched fingertips, and Kenny caught it for another big gain.

Finally, I decided it was time for my favorite play.

"We're going for it," I said in the huddle, trying to sound like Chad Pennington, quarterback of the real Jets.

"We're too far away," Kenny squealed.

Not listening to him, I turned toward Bobby and said, "Fade-out, fade-in bomb."

"No-o-o," Kenny whined, angrily pushing his big glasses up the bridge of his long, narrow nose.

"Whatta ya mean 'no-o-o'?" I bellowed. Hey, I was the quarterback, captain, and coach of the team.

"We've run that play twice already," Kenny said.

"And completed it both times," I said right back.

"They're expecting you to throw that," Mikey said. "Try something different."

Kirby called from the scrimmage line, "Are you jerks ready?"

"We're ready," I yelled back. I gave my players a fierce quarterback look and said, "Fade-out, fade-in bomb. Let's go."

I clapped my hands hard, just like Chad Pennington did on every big play, and led them up to the line. We got into formation and I started the play.

"Hike!" I yelled.

Carl Kaplan started yelling "Mississippis" so loud they could maybe hear him across the river in New York, and I dropped back really fast, my heart racing.

First, I looked left toward Kenny, hoping to sucker the Giants into covering him tight.

Then I turned back toward Mikey, who was moving his bulky body toward the big tree that marked out-of-bounds.

Finally, I looked over the middle. Bobby was wide open, fading in where the brown patch of grass marked the end zone. I gripped the ball, pulled my arm way back, and let her fly with all the strength my undersized body could muster.

As the ball reached its highest point against the blue sky, I knew it was a perfect pass. I watched it slowly start to come down, and down, and down to what would be a historic catch and a sure touchdown. The ball was about to fall into Bobby's bony, open hands—when Kirby Carpenter jumped in front of him and stole the ball away.

"No!" I yelled.

Kirby started galloping upfield. Bobby tried to catch him, but Kirby's long legs left Bobby behind. Then Kirby whipped past Kenny and Mikey, who just stood there looking like they didn't know what was going on.

I ran sideways, jumping over clumps of dead grass, my eyes glued to Kirby.

Carl Kaplan was out in front blocking for Kirby. He tried to push me away, but I gave him the strongest shove I could manage, and he fell hard to the ground. Then it was just Kirby and me. He rushed toward me at racecar speed.

Now's the time, I thought to myself. Make your move.

I lunged at Kirby, both arms outstretched, ready to

two-hand touch him and stop him from scoring. But just as I lunged, he stepped to his right and roared around me as I fell face-first into a clump of dead grass.

"Thirty-five! We win!" Kirby crowed from the end zone, as I lay on the ground, wishing I were anyplace but McNally Park, Hartsburg, New Jersey.

I felt feet clomping toward me, so I pulled my head from the dirt and looked up. It was Kirby and his smirking teammates.

"Good game, Paulsen," he said, sneering down at me. "You can't help it you guys stink." He and his team broke into hysterical laughter that made me want to punch each and every one of them.

"See you later," he went on, spiking the ball into the dirt right in front of my face.

As we slumped out of the park, none of my teammates said a thing. Part of me wanted to yell and jump up and down until I made a hole as big as a house in the sidewalk. But another part of me just wanted to hide. I held on tight to my dirty, cut-up football, and walked on silently, staring down at the grimy, gray pavement.

Finally, Bobby piped up.

"You know, we did pretty well."

"Huh?" Kenny said.

"Thirty-five to fourteen," Bobby said. "Better than last time."

"Last time we didn't score at all!" Kenny snapped.

"That's what I mean," Bobby said, nodding.

"We could have gotten more points," Kenny insisted.

"Yeah," Mikey said, nodding his huge head in agreement with Kenny.

"We might have even won the game," Kenny went on, "if we hadn't thrown that dumb pass."

I didn't want to hide anymore. "What dumb pass?" I demanded.

"The fade-out, fade-in bomb," Kenny said, adjusting his glasses.

"Yeah," Mikey agreed.

"It's a good play," I defended myself.

"It's a good play if you call it once a game," Kenny shot back. "You call it three, four, five times."

"I call down-and-outs a lot more," I said, sure that I had him.

"Down-and-outs aren't as risky," he said, shooting a "duh" look to the other guys. "The bomb goes right over the middle. It's the easiest pass in the world to intercept."

He had me there. Had me so good that there was nothing I could say to defend myself. So I did what I always did in situations like that—I said something stupid.

"You just don't like the play 'cause I don't throw it to you," I snapped at Kenny.

"What?!" he yelled.

"You don't like it 'cause I throw it to Bobby. The bomb is Bobby's play."

"Yeah, it's my play," Bobby said, sticking up for me.

"I hate that play 'cause it's risky, and you call it too much, and it loses us games," Kenny said in one breath. "You make too many mistakes, Eddie. You shouldn't be quarterback all the time. You should give Mikey or me a chance. Maybe we'd win a game for a change."

"You guys can't throw," I shot back. "I can throw longer than you two put together. And I'm the coach. The coach says who gets to quarterback the team."

"Maybe we need a new coach," Kenny answered. "We lost because of you. You just won't admit it."

"Get outta here!" I yelled.

"No problem," Kenny said. "Come on, Mikey."

"Yeah. Take him with you," I said, waving my hand at Kenny's wimpy friend.

"Loser!" Kenny called as he and Mikey turned their backs on Bobby and me. They lumbered toward Arlington Street.

"You're both losers," I called back.

"Losers!" Bobby seconded.

Bobby and I stood there for a few minutes without saying a thing to each other. We watched them until they got so small we could barely see them. I was already starting to feel lousy for what I'd said. But Kenny was right about one thing—I didn't like to admit when I was wrong.

I turned toward Bobby. "Let's go," I said, and we started walking up Boswell Road. "They're really something," I said, still angry. "Always complaining."

"Yeah, all they do is complain," Bobby agreed.

"We coulda won that game if they'd tried harder. I mean, when Kirby was running the interception back, he ran right past Kenny. And Mikey didn't even make a move."

"Nope."

"They're not interested in football anymore. All Kenny cares about is computers. And all Mikey cares about is girls."

"Yeah. Girls," Bobby said, making a face.

"How are your arms?"

"Pretty good," Bobby replied, pulling up his sleeves.

I looked at his arms really close. They looked like miniature versions of a roadmap—all lines and dots and blotches of blue, black, and red.

"Hurt?" I asked.

"Nah. Just that cut there," he said, pointing to a long, red gash.

"Bad?"

"Nah. My sister will take care of it. She's practicing for when she becomes a doctor."

"She's really smart," I said, thinking of Bobby's twin sister Jackie.

"Yeah. I guess," Bobby replied, staying with me step-for-step.

"Maybe she could help us with new plays," I joked.

"Our plays are good, Eddie," Bobby said, "no matter what Kenny and Mikey say."

After Bobby turned onto Eldridge Street, I stayed on Boswell Road, still mad about losing the game, and even madder for acting like a jerk with Kenny and Mikey. Not that I was completely wrong. The truth was they didn't seem to care much about football anymore. And I really didn't understand that, because football is the most important thing in my life. Not just football. Jets football.

See, I was born in Queens, New York, where the Jets started out a really long time ago in the 1960s. We moved to Hartsburg six years ago so my father could work in the body shop that his brother, my Uncle Joey, had just opened. My dad and Uncle Joey grew up in Queens, too, and they'd been telling me stories since I was little about the great Jets teams.

Okay, so there weren't many great Jets teams. In fact, there were very few. But my dad always says it's easy to back a winner. Backing a team that doesn't win is difficult. He says it builds character—and character is the most important thing in life.

Even though the Jets have played in New Jersey for more years than I've been alive, the only kids in school who like them are Bobby, Kenny, Mikey, and I. Everybody else is a Giants fan. And the meanest, stupidest, most loudmouthed Giants fan of all is Kirby Carpenter. That's why I got the team together.

Ever since we were little, it seemed like Kirby and I always had played against each other. Even though I'm kind of small, I have a strong arm. So I was always quarterbacking one side, and he was always quarterbacking the other. And he beat me every single time. Sure, I got close once or twice, but Kirby always found a way to score at the last minute. Every time, he used his loud mouth to say mean stuff about me. I hated Kirby Carpenter. I had to find a way to beat him at football—maybe that would shut him up once and for all.

One day it hit me. If I practiced and played with the same guys, we might get good enough to beat him. So last year I got a team together: Bobby, Kenny, Mikey, and me. I challenged Kirby to play against my new team, the Jets. He accepted and called his team the Giants. We made it a regular thing, every Saturday at 11 a.m., from September until Christmas. Even though we haven't beaten him yet, we've had some real close games. That tells me we can beat him. It's just a matter of time. And that's going to be the best day of my life.

I turned onto Juniper Street, feeling like I always did after losing to Kirby: sweaty, dirty, and angry. Usually when I got home, my dad was in the driveway waxing his car. I'd throw him the ball and tell him about the entire game, play by play, describing exactly how we could have won if only we'd done something a little differently. And he'd tell me that as long as I played my best, I shouldn't be upset.

I took the ball in my hands to get ready to throw it to him. Then I noticed the garage door was shut, and he wasn't there. So I stopped and looked around the yard to see if he was clipping bushes or raking leaves. After a few seconds of looking, I lowered the ball to my hip and headed into the house through the back door.

"You're home," my mom said as she took a bottle of disinfectant from under the sink and began to spray the kitchen countertop. "How'd you do?"

"Lost."

"Bad?"

"Thirty-five to fourteen," I said.

"That's not so bad," Mom said.

"Where's Dad?" I asked.

"He didn't feel so well, so he's lying down."

"Is he sick?"

"He said his nose was running. But I don't think it's much. Still, don't go near him. If he does have something, I don't want you to get it."

"Okay."

"I do want you to go get a shower," she said, wrinkling up

her nose. "You're filthy."

"I was playing football," I insisted.

"You're home now," she said, giving me one of her firm looks. "Clean yourself up, or no TV."

"I need a drink first," I said, pulling open the refrigerator door and grabbing a soda. I popped open the can and put it directly to my lips, something my mom didn't like me to do.

When I lowered the can, I saw her staring right at me, her eyes as cold as the can in my dirty hand.

"I was thirsty," I apologized.

"Shower. Now," she commanded.

"Okay," I said and headed upstairs. At least a shower might make me feel better.

Chapter Two

QUARTERBACK SNEAK

The next day was Sunday, and my dad was feeling a lot better. In fact, he was feeling so good that he decided to go to church, which was something he didn't do very much, even though my mom took me every week whether I liked it or not.

"I don't know if it was a cold or an allergy," Dad said at breakfast, "but I feel good and I'm gonna go."

But I wasn't thinking much about church right then. What I was thinking was that the real Jets were playing the Patriots that afternoon, and I was sure they had a good chance to pull off an upset.

I made it through church, and said a quick prayer for the Jets. When I got home, I finished my homework, which meant reading a section about Paul Revere from my Famous Americans in History textbook. It said in the chapter that he was a patriot. I thought about football.

It took almost forever, but the clock finally hit 4:00 p.m. I ran downstairs, clicked on the TV, and jumped onto the couch just as the announcer said, "Welcome to Giants

Stadium in the Meadowlands."

I cringed when I heard the name "Giants Stadium." I always did. After all, it's the Jets' home field, too.

"Today it's the New England Patriots versus the New York Jets," the announcer went on.

"Yeah!" I yelled, pumping my fist in the air. Then I looked toward the kitchen. "Hey, Dad. Where are you? The game's gonna start."

"Hold on a second, Mister," he called back in his big. game-day voice. "I'm coming."

He made it to the couch in time for the kick-off, a Coke in one hand and a bag of pretzels in the other.

"What are we gonna do today?" he called out, his face one huge smile.

"Win!" I called back, sticking my hand into the bag and pulling out a fistful.

"Don't eat too many or your mother will get mad," he warned me.

But I didn't even say anything back to him, because the New England kicker had just booted the ball, and the game had started for real.

On the first series of downs, the Jets went nowhere and had to punt. New England got the ball and marched down the field for a touchdown.

The next time the Jets got the ball, Chad Pennington

threw an interception, and the New England cornerback ran it right into the end zone. The game was hardly five minutes old, and already the score was 14-0.

"This doesn't look so good," I groaned to my father.

"Huh? Oh. It's still early," he mumbled, downing his soda.

When the first quarter ended, the score was 28-0. I was so depressed that when the front door opened and Uncle Joey and Aunt Lori walked in, I looked up from the TV, which was something I hardly ever did during a Jets game.

"Not doing so well, are they?" Uncle Joey said.

"Nope," I said.

Then the announcer said something that snapped me right back to the TV: "Looks like they're taking out Pennington and putting in Brooks Bollinger."

I looked hard at the screen. How could that be true? But it was. Chad Pennington was coming out and back-up quarterback Brooks Bollinger was going in. And the weirdest thing was . . . it worked. The second quarter was all Jets. Bollinger threw four touchdown passes, each more than twenty yards. In no time the game was tied, and I was feeling like it was my birthday and Christmas all on the same day.

"It looks like a new team out there," said the announcer. "I guess if the Jets want to win today, they've got to go with somebody new."

And that's when it all clicked.

"A new team."

"Somebody new."

That's what I would have to do to beat Kirby Carpenter. Get a new team.

"Dinner!" Mom called, snapping me out of my dream.

I turned and saw that she and Aunt Lori were placing plates of steaming food on the dining room table.

"Where's your father?" Mom asked me.

I looked up and saw that I was alone. I hadn't even heard him leave.

"I don't know," I said, feeling really dumb.

"Look outside. And if he's there, tell him everything's ready."

"And if your uncle's with him, tell him to come in, too," Aunt Lori said.

I ran over to the front door, all excited over my plan to beat Kirby, not to mention the Jets' comeback. I threw the door open and saw Dad and Uncle Joey standing in the shadow of the garage.

"Dinner's ready!" I called. "You're supposed to come in."

"Be right there!" Uncle Joey called back without turning toward me.

I slammed the door shut and ran upstairs to wash. On my way to the bathroom I wondered for about a half a second whether my dad was feeling sick again, because when I looked out the door I saw he had his hands to his eyes and was rubbing both of them really hard.

All through dinner and the rest of the game (which the Jets actually won), I thought about building a new team. I even daydreamed about throwing touchdown passes to new players who would actually want to play with me. I have to say I completely stopped feeling bad about how I'd treated Kenny and Mikey. The only thing that mattered to me now was starting over and beating Kirby.

As soon as I made it to school the next day, I found Bobby and went over to tell him the idea.

"A new team?!" he yelled.

"Ssshhh," I said, putting my hand over his mouth.

"What do you mean a new team?"

"I mean a new team. You and me and two new guys."

"No Kenny and Mikey?"

"No Kenny and Mikey."

"Wow," he said, his eyes wide.

"You saw what happened yesterday," I told him. "Brooks Bollinger went in, and the Jets won. The announcer said it was like a whole new team out there."

"He did," Bobby said, nodding.

"So that's what we've gotta do."

"But is it legal?"

"Of course it's legal. I started the team. I can change it."

"Who are you gonna ask to play?"

Without even thinking, I said, "Maybe the two new guys in class."

"Marty and Sean?"

"Yeah. Nobody ever plays with them," I said, nodding toward the far corner of the yard where they stood by themselves. "And they're both pretty big. I bet they could knock Kirby down with no problem."

"How are you gonna tell Kenny and Mikey?" Bobby asked, nervously pushing his bony hand through his wavy black hair.

"I don't know," I admitted, "but I'm gonna. Just don't say anything, okay?"

"I don't know a thing," he said, shaking his head.

All that morning I stared across the classroom at Kirby Carpenter. I remembered an interview Brooks Bollinger gave right after he was drafted. He said that he always tried to psych-out middle linebackers by staring at them when he called signals. So that's what I did to Kirby. Even when Ms. Gregg called on me to talk about Paul Revere, I answered her questions while giving Kirby a long, hard, cold stare.

When Ms. Gregg let us go to lunch, Kirby came over looking like an angry pit bull. "What's your problem?" he barked down at me.

"I don't have a problem," I barked back.

"Still mad 'cause we kicked your butt?"

"It's the last time you kick my butt."

"Yeah, right," he said and chuckled.

"Look what the Jets did yesterday," I said.

"Big deal. They won thirty-five to thirty-one."

"The Giants only scored twenty-one points," I said, sure that I had him.

"But they won by eleven," Kirby said with a smirk. "The Jets only won by four."

I thought hard for a really good comeback, but before I could think of something sharp to say, he laughed at me and lumbered out of the room.

After Bobby and I finished eating lunch, we headed for the schoolyard to play catch. We were sixth graders, so the younger kids didn't get in the way when we took a prime piece of the yard to play on. I always took a section near the fence and didn't let anybody trespass for any reason.

"You decide how you're gonna do it?" Bobby called as he threw me the ball.

"Ssshhh," I said as I caught the ball and flipped it back in a perfect spiral.

"You're all the way over there," he said. "You won't hear me if I whisper."

"I'll hear you," I told him. "Don't yell."

"You decide how you're gonna do it?" he whispered.

"No," I whispered back. "But I'm working on it."

Then Bobby whispered something else, but I couldn't understand what he was saying.

"What?" I said.

"I told you you wouldn't hear me."

"Everybody's making too much noise," I said, nodding toward the third grade girls who were screaming as they jumped rope nearby.

"Kenny and Mikey will probably be mad," Bobby said.

"Probably," I agreed. "But what am I gonna do?"

"I don't know," Bobby said, shrugging and then throwing me the ball.

"Look around the yard. Do you see Kenny anywhere?" I said.

Bobby looked around, then turned back to me, and shook his head.

"As soon as he's done eating, he goes right to the computer room. And take a look over there," I said, pointing toward the far corner of the yard where Mikey was talking with red-haired Dana McAllister. "How are we gonna win a football game hanging around with girls?"

"We're not."

"You got it," I said, throwing him the ball. "It's just gotta be us. A team. Nothing else."

"Yeah," Bobby agreed, catching it one-handed and flinging it right back to me. "And if I were Mikey, I'd be careful around Dana McAllister. Her brother is in junior high, and he probably wouldn't like it if he knew Mikey was hanging out with his sister."

"Probably not."

"Matt Weller came over to my house two weeks ago looking for my sister. She wasn't home. But I told him he better not come back."

"Yeah?"

"Yeah. I also told him if I saw him following her around the schoolyard, I'd beat him up."

"Would you?"

"Yeah. I don't want anybody to try to date my sister," he declared. "I don't know why anybody would want to. But they better not."

Bobby flipped me the ball real hard. I caught it and flipped it back, low to the ground. He grabbed it, hit the cement, and came up smiling.

The only thing on my mind all week was how I was going to tell Kenny and Mikey I didn't want them on the team anymore. Part of me thought I should just sit them down and talk to them. Since they had no interest in football anymore, they probably wouldn't care if I cut them. But the other part of me knew we'd get into a huge argument, and maybe even a fist fight, because they wouldn't want to be kicked off the team, no matter how uninterested they were.

I wanted to ask my father what he would do. But he worked late at the shop every night, and by the time he got home, I was always finishing up my homework and heading for bed. I thought about asking my mother. But every time I tried, her cell phone rang, or she was online, or she was doing whatever a wife, mom, and part-time administrative assistant at an insurance company does.

Finally, on Thursday my dad got home a little earlier, and I waited in the living room for him until he finished his dinner.

"Are you sure you want to change the team?" he asked me, looking really serious.

"I'm sure, Dad," I said back.

"Why?"

"I wanna beat Kirby."

"You've been playing with Kenny and Mikey for a long time."

"They cut players all the time in the NFL."

"This isn't the NFL," he said, his expression not changing.

"I guess. But we're not even friendly anymore. They don't talk to me much at school. We don't even play catch at lunchtime."

"I'm not saying you shouldn't do this. Sometimes you have to make a change. Being a coach and captain means making tough decisions—it's not easy."

"No kidding."

"Who are you going to replace them with?"

"There are these two new guys. Marty and Sean. Just moved to the neighborhood. They look pretty good in gym class. I think they can play."

"Well, before you tell Kenny and Mikey, make sure Marty and Sean want to be on the team," he suggested. Then he stretched his arms way out from his body and yawned as wide as a tunnel. "It's getting late, Mister. I think we'd both better hit the sack."

The next day I did exactly what he said. As soon as I got to school I went over to Marty and Sean and asked them if they wanted to play with Bobby and me. And they were both glad I asked them. They smiled as bright as lights at Giants Stadium during a night game.

But I still didn't know how I was going to tell Kenny and Mikey. While I was standing by myself in the middle of the schoolyard trying to think of a way, Kirby Carpenter came over, smirking like he owned the world.

"I'm not playing against you guys this week," he told me. "I wanna play against a real team."

"Well, I'm not gonna play against you guys for a few weeks," I said right back, staring up at him as hard as I could. "I've gotta practice with my new team."

"New team?" he asked, his eyes opening really wide. "You can't have a new team."

"Who says?"

"I say."

"This isn't the NFL," I shot back.

"We've been playing each other for over a year. Every time, same team. You can't change now."

And then out of nowhere I said something without thinking.

"I can't keep the same team when two players quit it."

"Who quit?"

"Kenny and Mikey," I said before I could think.

"They're smart," Kirby sneered.

"Smart or not, they quit. So I get to pick new players."

"Good luck. Anybody who'd want to play with you is a moron," he said and stomped away.

All day I felt awful that I had said something untrue about Kenny and Mikey. Really awful. I wasn't thinking straight when I said it. Whenever I try to keep up with Kirby

Carpenter, my brain acts weird. Sometimes it doesn't work at all. Other times it works too fast. And when my brain works too fast, sometimes I say things that aren't exactly . . . true. I thought hard all day about how to take back what I'd said. But by the time school was over, I hadn't come up with a thing. If I'd known what was going to happen next, I would have thought a lot harder.

I had just left school and was walking up Elwell Road with Bobby when I heard my name called. I turned and saw Kenny and Mikey coming toward me. From the way they were breathing, I knew they had either eaten the hottest chili peppers in the world, or they had heard about what I'd said to Kirby.

"We just heard something," Kenny called, taking T-Rex-sized steps toward me.

"Oh, yeah?" I said, trying to sound innocent. "What?"

"We just heard we quit the team."

"Wait a second—"

"In fact," said Kenny, "we heard from Kirby Carpenter that we quit the team. Right, Mikey?"

"Yeah," Mikey said.

"There's only one problem, Eddie," Kenny continued. "I don't remember us quitting the team. Do you, Mikey?"

"Nope, I sure don't," Mikey said with a scowl.

"So how could we have quit the team, if we don't remember

quitting it?" Kenny asked.

"Okay. I know you didn't quit the team," I said, hoping to buy time.

"You bet we didn't quit the team," Kenny shot right back.

"It just came out. It was an accident."

"It was an accident," Bobby said.

"No way," Kenny insisted. "You want us off the team."

"I-I don't want you off the team," I said weakly.

"Tell the truth, Eddie," Kenny challenged me. "You want us off the team."

I took a quick breath, and then admitted everything. "Okay. I want you off the team."

"You're a—" Kenny started.

"It's not like you're interested in football anymore," I accused him.

"Who says we're not interested in football?" asked Kenny.

"All you're interested in is computers. And, Mikey, all you're interested in is girls."

"Computers are important," Kenny insisted.

"Yeah. And so are girls," Mikey added.

"And just because we like other things doesn't mean we don't like football," Kenny continued.

"You never try very hard," I snapped.

"What?!" Kenny yelled.

"When Kirby intercepted my pass, you guys didn't do a thing."

"We shouldn't have had to do a thing," Kenny said, breathing so hard his glasses were getting fogged up. "You shouldn't have thrown that stupid pass."

"It wasn't a stupid pass."

"It lost us the game. You're always losing us games."

"Then why do you even want to be on my team?" I asked. I had him at last.

"We don't!" Kenny shouted right at me. "We're gonna make our own team. And we're gonna beat Kirby Carpenter and make you look like the jerk and liar you are."

Kenny then turned toward Mikey and yelled a quick "let's go!" They broke through the crowd of kids that had formed around us. I watched half of my team storm down Elwell Road.

I looked around at the kids who were standing there. At least twenty pairs of eyes stared at me. And behind those pairs of eyes were brains, all thinking, "Liar . . . Jerk." I wanted to shout something that could clear my name. But my brain wasn't working again. Besides, I knew it wouldn't do me any good.

After a few really long moments—the type when you're waiting for the referee to decide whether your team made a close first down or not—the crowd broke up, and Bobby and

I headed up Elwell Road. After walking a block in silence, Bobby uttered a soft, bewildered "wow."

"Yeah. Wow," I echoed.

Chapter Three

WALKOUT

It was a really cool October day when my new team first met to practice. The sun was out and a cold breeze rustled the leaves that were just starting to turn yellow.

"Football weather," my dad always said. "When the leaves start to turn, it's football weather."

Bobby and I were the first to show up that Saturday afternoon. First, we talked about some new plays I'd come up with, which included a midfield crossing pattern and a modified flea flicker, because Sean told me that he had a good arm. I threw a few low ones to Bobby while we waited. In no time he was slamming into the dirt and smiling like crazy.

Eventually Marty showed up, chewing nervously on a wad of bubble gum. But we waited another half hour for Sean, who got his hair cut so short it looked like he was almost bald.

"Where were you?" I called over to him as he stepped out of his mother's car, stumbled, and nearly fell to the ground.

"Sorry I'm late, guys," he apologized. "I had to get my hair cut."

"I can tell," I replied, wanting to chew him out really bad. This was our first practice, so I decided I'd better not. Instead, I growled, "Let's get started," in the strongest quarterback voice I could manage and led them all to the middle of the field.

I started with down-and-outs. First to Bobby. Then to Sean.

But when I threw one to Marty, the ball slipped right through his hands.

"Sorry, Eddie," he called to me, chewing hard on his gum and looking embarrassed.

"It's okay. Let's try again," I called back.

Again I threw down-and-outs. Bobby. Sean.

"Here it comes, Marty!" I called.

But the ball slipped through his hands again.

"The ball feels slippery," he said, chewing even faster.

"Are your hands clean?" I asked with a scowl.

"I think so."

"Well, make sure. Okay?"

He gave both hands a quick look, rubbed them on his jeans, and nodded at me.

The rest of the practice went the same way. Marty didn't catch so well, and Sean couldn't run or throw. He was constantly tripping—and not only over clumps of dead grass. He also tripped over his own two elephant-sized feet, hitting the ground each time with a loud "thud." And when we tried the flea flicker, his "strong arm" barely got the ball halfway to Bobby downfield.

"I need a little more practice," he told me, nervously running his hand through the few hairs on his head.

"It's okay," I said, trying my best to keep smiling. "You're gonna get it."

After practice, as Bobby and I were walking home, he asked, "What do you think?"

"What do you think?" I asked back.

Bobby paused for a second.

"They're nice guys," he finally said.

"Yeah. They are."

"Marty runs fast," Bobby offered.

"Yeah."

"And Sean can catch."

"He can."

"And they don't have anybody to play with."

"After a few practices, they're gonna be real good," I declared.

"Even better than Kenny and Mikey, maybe," Bobby said.

"Yeah. Maybe."

We separated at the end of the street without saying another word.

When I got home, I saw my dad's car in the driveway. I

walked into the house and called out, "Hey, Dad!" But there was no reply. Then I saw that the back door was open. I pushed open the screen door and headed into the yard. Standing in the middle of the lawn, looking toward the back fence, was my dad.

"Dad," I called.

He didn't move.

"Dad!" I said a little louder.

He still didn't move.

"Hey, Dad!" I finally yelled.

He turned with a start.

"Hey, Mister. How's it going?" he called to me, breaking into a big smile.

"Great," I called back. "What are you doing?"

"Just thinking."

"What about?" I asked, heading toward him.

"A lot of stuff. You look good," he said, looking down at my dirty clothes. "Why don't you go wash up? I'll come in in a few minutes."

Then I noticed his eyes were all red.

"Are you okay?" I asked.

"Sure I am," he replied.

"Your eyes—"

"That's just allergies," he broke in. "Now go inside. I'll be right there."

I stood watching him for a few more seconds. But I could tell he didn't want me to stay in the yard with him, so I turned around and went back into the house.

I was heading upstairs when the front door opened, and my mom came in. Her leather bag was slung over her shoulder, and the handles of two overstuffed grocery bags were in each hand.

"Take these," she said, extending the bags in her right hand straight at me.

"You got it," I said, taking the bags from her.

"Where's your father?"

"In the backyard."

"He's not watering, is he?" she wondered out loud, lowering the other two bags onto the counter and lifting her face toward the window. "He shouldn't be watering."

"He's not watering. He's sneezing."

"What's wrong with him now?" she said, almost as if I weren't there.

"Is there something the matter with him?" I asked, starting to feel really nervous.

"Eddie, don't ask me silly questions. Here," she said, pushing one of the two bags on the counter toward me. "It's soap and toothpaste. Take them up to the bathroom."

"What do you want me to do with these?" I asked, lifting the two bags I was holding.

"Leave those down here. Take that one upstairs. Go!"

My mom pushed open the back door and headed into the yard. I stood there, two grocery bags in one hand and another bag close to me on the counter. Finally, I did what my mom said. I put down the two bags I was holding and took the soap and toothpaste up to the bathroom. As I headed upstairs, I was sure that no quarterback in the NFL had to put away soap and toothpaste. They had people working for them whose only job was to handle the soap and toothpaste. In my house that was me. True, I wasn't in the NFL yet. But some day . . .

When I made it up to the bathroom, I looked at myself in the mirror. A huge clump of stick-straight brown hair fell over my forehead. I took my right hand and pushed it back. Would this face someday appear in the sports pages of newspapers around the country? I sure hoped so.

My new team needed all the practice it could get, so the next week I tried to get the guys together as much as possible. But it wasn't easy.

On Monday Sean couldn't come.

On Tuesday Marty couldn't come.

On Wednesday it was Bobby who couldn't make it.

And on Thursday it rained.

Finally, I thought everybody would be there Friday. But Bobby and I waited at the park for a half hour, and neither Marty nor Sean showed.

"They told me they were gonna be here," I complained.

"Maybe Sean fell and hurt himself," Bobby suggested with a grin.

"Maybe Marty swallowed his gum," I replied, grinning, too.

Bobby and I burst into laughter, and it seemed to go on forever. For the first time in days, I felt like everything would turn out just fine. After we settled down, Bobby and I started practicing by ourselves.

I threw short passes to him and then long ones. High ones and low ones. And he didn't miss a single catch.

I'd been playing sports with Bobby since first grade. I met him right after his parents got divorced. He was really quiet and really small and a lot of kids made fun of him. We got to be friends by playing catch in the schoolyard. We played punchball, then baseball, and even basketball. But when we started playing football together, we became best friends. Bobby was the wiriest kid in school, and when I threw to him, it was like my passes were laser-guided. I liked coming up with down-and-outs and down-and-ins with weird motions and movements made just for him. And he loved it whenever I had a new play.

As I was thinking back on some of those crazy plays I'd come up with, I threw a ball way out to the side. Bobby lunged for it, his arms like two baseball bats, they were so straight. He grabbed the ball, but then hit the ground hard, slid for a few inches, and let out a sharp, "Owww!"

"Are you okay?" I called, running over to him.

"I think," he groaned.

"You're bleeding," I said.

"It's okay," he replied, struggling up from the ground.

"It's not okay."

"It is so! I've had worse cuts," he said, handing me the ball. "Let's play."

"That's a big cut."

"It's not."

"It is," I insisted, grabbing his arm to show him. But as soon as I touched him he let out another "owww!" and pulled away.

"We're not gonna keep playing. You should probably go to the doctor."

"I'm not going to the doctor for a little cut."

"Then you're going home."

"Okay. I'm going home," he growled, turning away from me angrily.

I walked Bobby to his house. Along the way he kept telling me he had stopped bleeding. But every time he took his hand away to show me, the blood was still oozing out.

When we got to his house on Eldridge Street, he opened the door and we went in. His mother was cutting chunks of fat off a steak in the kitchen.

"Home so early?" she said. "Did you finally get tired of football?"

Bobby held up his arm, and his mother dropped her knife as if the handle were on fire. She quickly washed her hands and rushed over to him.

"What happened?" she cried.

"I cut myself. I'm okay," he told her, pulling away.

"You're not okay if you cut yourself."

"It's not even bleeding anymore. Just give me a Band-Aid."

"You need more than a Band-Aid. You need peroxide. That cut is filthy!"

"That's gonna make it sting," Bobby squealed.

"That means it's clean. Give me your arm," she said, trying to grab his other arm.

Then I heard a voice from over my shoulder.

"Let me do it, Mom," the voice said.

I turned and saw Bobby's sister Jackie standing in the kitchen doorway. And I instantly felt really weird. I say "weird" because I felt a combination of things, none of which I'd ever felt all at the same time before.

I felt tingly, like when my foot falls asleep when I sit on it for too long. And I felt sweaty, like the temperature in the room went up really fast.

Then Bobby said something, and Jackie replied. But I didn't hear what they were saying. I was too focused on Jackie—her brown eyes, her tan skin, and her shoulder-length black hair.

Jackie led Bobby upstairs, and I followed.

She took him into the bathroom, sat him down on the edge of the tub, and washed his cut with a damp cloth. Bobby kept saying "owww" every time she touched him, but for the first time in my life, I wished I had been cut. I didn't know why, but I wanted to be sitting where he was, my arm all red with dried blood, with Jackie Rodriguez wiping it clean.

After she had finished washing his arm, she poured on some peroxide. Bobby yelled so loud I thought his arm was broken, not just cut. Jackie bandaged him up and announced, "You can go. I'll send you a bill." Then she looked over and tossed me a smile.

He turned to her, looking a little embarrassed, and grunted, "Thanks, Doc." He stood up and took a step to leave the bathroom, but I was standing in the doorway and wouldn't let him out. It wasn't that I wanted to keep him there. It was just that my body was still tingling and my feet and legs seemed to be going numb.

"Let's go, Eddie," Bobby said, trying to nudge me out of the way.

"Sorry," I said as I finally got back my strength and moved to let him pass.

As Jackie washed her hands, covering them with a mountain of suds, I just stood there watching her, feeling weak and excited all at the same time.

"Do you want a Coke or a root beer?" Bobby called from downstairs.

"You did a great job," I said to her, totally without thinking.

She looked up at me, giggled just a little, and said, "Thanks."

"Do you want a Coke or a root beer?" Bobby called again, this time much louder.

"Coke," I called back, not really caring either way, perfectly happy just to stand there and watch Jackie rub her hands back and forth as the steaming water poured over them.

I walked home still feeling weird. I kept moving one foot in front of the other, but I could hardly feel the sidewalk. I was holding my football in my right hand, my fingertips still tingling. And it all started when I saw Jackie standing in the kitchen doorway.

It's not like it was the first time I'd ever seen Jackie Rodriguez. I'd known her almost as long as I'd known Bobby. I just never paid much attention to her. One of the reasons was that she was always in the gifted students' class, while Bobby and I were always in the not-so-gifted students' class. Jackie had always been friendly to me. She always offered me a soda when I came to her house, she smiled at me in the hall at school, and she never made fun of me, unlike a lot of the other girls in the gifted class. But she was a girl and I was a guy. She had her own girl friends, and I had my own guy friends. She wanted to become a doctor, and I wanted to become a football player. We had nothing in common. She was just this skinny, straight-haired kid who knew a lot of stuff and giggled a lot. Now, out of nowhere, she was different. And she made me feel different, too. I wasn't sure how I felt about feeling so different, but the closer I got to my house, the more I thought I liked it.

I was still in a fog as I walked up the front steps. When I got inside, I heard shouting coming from upstairs. At first I thought it was my parents' bedroom TV, but when I listened harder, I could tell it was my mom and dad arguing. The tingling vanished.

I made it halfway up the stairs before I could make out what they were saying.

"What do you mean 'a new life'?" my mother asked.

"Just what it sounds like," my father replied.

"What's wrong with the life you have?" she asked, sounding angry.

"I'm thirty-nine years old. I'll be forty in a couple of months."

"So?"

"So, I work in my brother's body shop."

"And I work in an office."

"I've never done anything. I've never seen anything."

"You have a home," Mom countered.

"Which I can barely pay the mortgage on."

"You have a family. Isn't that enough?"

"I don't know. I thought by now I'd have a lot more."

I didn't want to hear any more. I stuck my fingers in my ears, ran downstairs, and hid in the kitchen. I could still hear their voices growing louder and louder, the bedroom door being thrown open, and footsteps above me. Then I saw my father tromp down the stairs. He was carrying a suitcase.

My mother came down right behind him, her cheeks all red like she'd been out in a snowstorm. He said something to her that I didn't hear, and then opened the front door and left. When the door slammed shut, I pulled my fingers from my ears and was dazed by the sound of my mother crying.

Chapter Four

PERFECT PASS

Later that afternoon my mom told me what had happened.

"Your dad's going to be spending a few days at Uncle Joey and Aunt Lori's," she said.

"Why?"

"He needs time to think."

"What about?"

"Things."

"What kind of things?"

"Just things," she said, looking like she was about to start crying again. "It's really hard to explain. I'll make you some hot dogs for dinner. I'm not really hungry."

I wasn't hungry either, but I nodded, and then headed upstairs to wash. I didn't feel weird anymore. I felt numb. I didn't want to talk, and I especially didn't want to cry. But when I closed the bathroom door, I couldn't hold in the hurt anymore. So it all came out. More tears than I'd ever cried—a whole lot more.

I tried to make it end, but I couldn't stop the tears. They

just poured out of me until none were left. Then I thought of my dad walking out, and I felt mad—madder than I'd ever felt at Kirby Carpenter or anybody else in my entire life.

That weekend took about a century to pass. Although I had scheduled practice both days, I had no interest in playing. At the end of Sunday's practice, Bobby asked me if I was feeling okay. I didn't really want to talk about it, but I remembered that my mom always said bad news travels fast. So I told him.

"My dad moved out."

"Oh, no," Bobby said, his eyes opening really wide.

"Oh, yeah," I admitted.

"Are they gonna get divorced?"

"I don't know," I replied, just the possibility making me really scared. "I don't think so."

"Did they fight a lot?"

"Some . . . Not much . . . Did your parents fight a lot?" I asked.

"I guess," Bobby said, looking away. "I can hardly remember my dad. I don't wanna remember my dad."

I wanted to start walking home, away from this conversation that was making me sadder and sadder.

"Did your mom cry?" Bobby turned to me and asked, his eyes black and intense.

"Yeah," I had to admit.

"My mom cried a lot, too," he said.

"Don't tell anybody. Okay?"

"No problem."

That evening my dad called up. I was hoping he and Mom would have a long talk, and then everything would be better, and he would come home. But that's not the way it happened.

"When are you coming back?" my mom demanded, her back turned to me.

She paused and then continued, "I cannot believe you. I don't want to talk anymore. Talk to your son. Tell him why you left."

My mom snapped around, shoved the phone at me, and said, "It's your father. He wants to talk to you."

I nervously took the phone from her as she stomped out of the kitchen and upstairs. But I wasn't really sure what I should do. Part of me didn't want to say a thing to him until I heard him apologize for making Mom cry. But another part of me wanted to talk to him really bad. So I stood there for a few long moments, then slowly raised the phone to my ear, and whispered, "Hello?"

"Hey, Mister. How are you doing?" my father said, sounding as if nothing strange had happened.

"I'm okay. How are you?" I managed to say.

"Working hard. Do your homework?"

"Yeah."

"Good. Watch the game?"

"Yeah."

"Rough game. But they only lost by three. And Pittsburgh's a tough team."

I didn't say a thing. Finally, he spoke again, this time much more softly.

"I'm sorry about not saying goodbye to you. I know it was wrong. But I had to go, and you weren't there. I hope you're not too mad at me."

It was then I thought he would say something about Mom. A sentence. A word. Something to make it all right. But he didn't say a thing. He just went back to his normal voice, like none of this was important.

"I'm gonna come over next Sunday. We'll watch the game together. Okay?"

I waited a few long moments, before I finally mumbled, "Okay."

"Great. Now work hard in class. And be good to your mother, okay?"

"I will," I mumbled again.

"Bye, Eddie."

Then I heard a click. The call was over.

I thought that whole week about what I would do when my dad came over on Sunday. Part of me wanted to ask him what he had gone off to think about. One thing was for sure—I wasn't going to show him how upset I was. And I definitely wasn't going to cry again.

I woke up Sunday feeling as nervous as a quarterback probably feels on the morning of the Super Bowl. I sat on the couch and stared at the dark TV screen.

"You didn't eat breakfast," Mom said, offering a paper plate filled with food. "Aren't you going to at least try to eat lunch?"

"I'm not hungry," I told her.

I thought she was going to keep on me. But she just walked away.

Finally, I heard a key in the front door. I clenched my fists and thought hard about the game.

Then the door opened, and my dad walked in.

"Hey," he said in his big, game-day voice, a broad smile across his face.

Mom didn't say a word.

"Hey, Jeanie. How are you?" my father asked.

"I'm fine, Tommy," she answered.

My mom took a few careful steps toward him, and he moved closer to her. When they met, he kissed her gently on the cheek.

Then Dad turned to me. "Hey, Mister," he said.

"Hey, Dad," I replied, barely getting the words out.

"Come give your old man a hug."

Right then all of my muscles tensed up. The last thing I wanted to do was give him a hug. At least that was the last thing the angry part of me wanted to do. But I was in a situation. My front line was collapsing, but I was already standing there, no one between me and the oncoming rush. There was nothing to do but get rid of the ball and take a hit. So I did. I let him come closer and wrap his arms around me. But I kept my arms at my sides.

My dad let go of me and went into the kitchen to get a Coke and a bag of pretzels. Then we got ready to watch the game. Today it was the Jets against the Bills. Usually I get really excited when we play Buffalo because they have a great offense. It takes everything the Jets have to keep it close. But I couldn't concentrate, no matter how hard I tried.

The Bills got the ball first, and they marched down the field until the Jets stopped them cold at the twenty-yard line. Buffalo had to settle for a field goal. Then it was the Jets' turn. Brooks Bollinger completed four straight passes, and in less than two minutes, the Jets were at midfield. Ordinarily, I would have been screaming like crazy after four completions. But I didn't say a word. All I could think of was that my father was sitting three feet away from me, and I wasn't sure if I wanted him there. I mean, if he couldn't be there every day, like he was supposed to, why should he be allowed to be there just because it was Sunday?

Right then Bollinger dropped back and threw a long one over the middle toward the wide receiver. But Buffalo's cornerback jumped up and intercepted the pass.

"Crap!" my father snapped, slapping his hand against his thigh. "We were almost there. Weren't we, Mister?"

"Yeah," I mumbled.

"But that was a risky pass," my dad continued. "Would you have called that play?"

I shrugged.

"Come on. You're the quarterback in the family," he went on, poking me in the shoulder.

I said nothing. My dad always talked more than I did during games, but right then it seemed that he was talking too much. I just shrugged again and kept looking at the TV.

We watched the game without saying too much until about midway through the second quarter. Then we smelled dinner cooking.

"Smells like chicken," Dad said.

"Yeah," I mumbled.

"I've always loved your mom's chicken," he went on.

I turned and looked up at him. My father's face looked really sad. Kind of like the face you see on a stray dog that's been outside in a rainstorm all day.

He looked at me with that face. "I'm sorry about what happened," he said. "I know I should have told you good-bye."

My throat began to tighten again, and I had a feeling that I might start crying. So I clenched my fists and tried to concentrate on the TV.

"I know you're probably mad," he continued. "I would be, too. Just don't be too mad."

"Why don't you come home?" The words just popped out.

"I can't," he said, shaking his head slightly. "Someday you'll understand."

Every muscle in my body tightened up. I wanted to punch everything near me, including him. Thankfully, I heard the click-clack of my mom's shoes against the dining room floor.

"Dinner," she said without much spirit.

"I'd better go wash up," I told Dad, and I jerked my body up off the couch and headed upstairs.

Dinner was awful. I barely swallowed a half of a chicken leg and four French fries. I never touched the asparagus. My dad ate well, though, and went on and on about the cars he was working on at the shop. My mom picked at her food and hardly looked up.

When the meal was over, Mom sent me to my room to do

my homework. After a few minutes, I heard them talking, so I silently opened my door just a crack. I had to hear what they were saying, even if it was something that would make me feel terrible.

"Thanks for the dinner," I heard my dad say. "The chicken was really good . . . I–uh–I'll call you."

"You're going?" Mom asked.

"It's late," Dad replied.

"You said nothing all night."

"I talked."

"You know what I mean," Mom said.

"Jeanie . . ."

"What's going on? You have responsibilities here."

"I know."

"You're not fulfilling them."

"I'm doing my best," he insisted.

"This is your best?" my mom demanded, her voice starting to crack.

"Right now, yeah. This is my best," he replied.

Part of me wanted to close the door, but I had to keep listening—even though I knew what I was going to hear wasn't going to make me happy.

"You can't just come in here, watch a football game, eat dinner, and leave," Mom said.

"Right now, that's all I can do," Dad replied.

"I don't understand you, Tommy."

"That's right. You don't."

Then I heard heavy footsteps and the front door being opened.

"I'll call you tomorrow," Dad said. "Tell Eddie I'll call."

I heard the front door shut, and Mom started to come up the stairs. I carefully closed my door so she wouldn't hear me. Then I curled up on my bed and buried my face in my pillow.

The next week I decided to start practicing seriously again. It wasn't that I felt like playing football. I started playing again because I was sick of thinking about what hadn't happened with my dad.

I wanted him to apologize to my mother.

He didn't.

I asked him to come home.

He said he couldn't.

The longer I thought about it, the more I was sure he was never coming back. So I didn't want to think about it anymore. And the only thing that could take my mind off my problems was football.

The first day back was bright and warm, more like summer than fall. Everybody seemed glad to be there, especially

Bobby, whose arm was almost completely healed.

I started by throwing some short passes. Amazingly not one ball was dropped. Bobby, Marty, Sean—they were all in the zone. I threw longer and longer, and pretty soon I forgot what was happening at home. It all began to feel right again.

"Go out for a long one, Bobby," I called.

"Sure, Eddie."

Bobby headed out across the grass, farther and farther, as the October sun hit me right in the eyes. But it didn't matter. I knew where he was running. So I pulled the ball back and threw it high and far. As it flew through the air, I knew it would hit him square in the chest. And it did. Perfect.

"Wow! You're throwing great!" Bobby called to me.

"Thanks," I called back.

"We're gonna beat everybody!"

Sean, Marty, and I broke into a loud cheer. Then we heard a car horn.

"It's my mom," Bobby said, looking past us.

I turned and saw Mrs. Rodriguez's Pontiac. Mrs. Rodriguez was waving from the driver's seat. Then I saw Jackie waving from the back seat.

And I began to feel weird all over again.

It wasn't like I had forgotten what had happened when I watched her fix Bobby's cut. But with my dad moving out, and then coming back to visit, Jackie Rodriguez hadn't been on my mind much. But now, here she was. The more I watched her wave at me, the weirder I felt.

"Let's go, Bobby," Mrs. Rodriguez called.

"Gotta go, guys. Sorry," Bobby apologized.

When we got to the car, Jackie rolled down her window.

"Hi, Eddie," she said.

My throat got all dry when I tried to say "Hi, Jackie" back. But I got it out the best I could.

"You guys going to win?" she asked me.

"I think so," I replied.

"You've got to win. If you don't, my brother will go crazy," she said, turning to Bobby and filling the car with laughter.

Then the car rolled away, and the three of us stood there. Marty and Sean started tossing the ball to each other. I was frozen in place.

"Ready, Eddie?" Sean asked.

"Oh. Yeah," I said, snapping back to life. "Go out for a long one."

As Sean headed out across the scruffy grass, I pulled the ball back and let it fly. I watched it spiral over and over and over, and I imagined Jackie's face, and heard Jackie's voice, and wished she were watching me play.

All the way home, I thought about Jackie. I stumbled up the front steps and pulled open the door. Mom was dusting the living room furniture.

"How was practice?" she asked without a smile.

I nearly blurted out, "It was great, because of Jackie, Jackie, Jackie!" But I caught myself just in time and mumbled, "It was good."

"Everybody show?"

I almost yelled, "Yeah! Especially Bobby's incredible sister, who makes me feel really weird!" Instead, I calmly answered, "They were all there."

"I'm glad you had fun," my mom said. "We're having spaghetti for dinner."

"Great," I replied. But I didn't care about the spaghetti. Only Jackie mattered, and I had to see her as soon as possible. So, without thinking, I asked, "Mom, can I go over to Bobby's house?"

"Why!"

"Uhhh . . ."

"Why?" she asked again.

"I want to do my homework with him."

"I just told you I was making spaghetti."

"I know, but . . ."

"And didn't you spend the afternoon with Bobby?"

"Yeah. But we were practicing."

"If homework was so important, you could have done it instead of play football. Now take a shower. Dinner will be ready in a half hour."

I did what she said and was at the table when the spaghetti, meat sauce, and salad were served.

"The spaghetti may be a little soggy. I'm sorry," she muttered.

I put a forkful into my mouth, chewed, and swallowed. It was soggy. After downing another mouthful, I asked, "How was work?"

"I survived," she replied.

"Bad day?"

"Like any day . . . I may need to look for another job."

"Why?" I asked, turning toward her.

"I need full-time hours. I can't get them at my office. So I have to start looking."

I stabbed a piece of lettuce with my fork and brought it up to my mouth. My hand shook. I put the piece of lettuce into my mouth and chewed. It was sour with vinegar.

During dinner Mom usually asked about school. If any tests were coming up. If any projects were due. But she said nothing, just stared down at her plate, her brown hair falling forward against her face. She slowly twirled some spaghetti on her fork, but did not move it toward her mouth.

"Want more?" she asked.

"No, thank you," I replied.

After helping her with the dishes, I headed upstairs to do my reading. But in the quiet of my room I started thinking about Jackie again. I couldn't go to Bobby's house, so I decided that hearing Jackie's voice would be the next best thing to seeing her face.

I tiptoed down the stairs and saw my mother on the couch reading the newspaper. The help-wanted ads, I guessed. So I carefully headed toward my parents' room, raised the phone from its base, and anxiously punched in Jackie's number.

One ring.

Then two.

Then a click.

"Hello?" Mrs. Rodriguez said on the other end.

I slammed the phone down, ran back to my room, and waited. After a few minutes passed, I decided to give it another try and returned to my parents' room.

I nervously pushed redial, hoping that Jackie would pick up this time.

One ring.

A second.

Another click.

"Hello?" Bobby said on the other end.

I slammed the phone down again and tore back into my

room. No more calls, I decided. I would get her e-mail address when I saw her at school and contact her that way.

I tried to do some of my reading homework, but I could barely concentrate on any of the words. I had to speak to Jackie. I knew I couldn't study, and I wasn't sure if I could even go to sleep if I didn't. So I headed back into my folks' bedroom and quickly called again.

"Hello?" Jackie answered.

"H-h-hello, Jackie," I stuttered. "It's Eddie."

"Eddie. Hi," she said, sounding so happy I knew she had to be smiling.

"How are you?" I asked.

"Good."

"It was nice seeing you at the park," I said.

"It was nice seeing you, too. How is the team doing?"

"Good. Bobby didn't cut himself today."

"No," she said and giggled. "But if he does, I'll take care of him. Do you want to talk to him?"

I wanted to say "no," but I didn't want Jackie to get suspicious, so I told her that I did. Bobby quickly picked up the phone.

"Hey, Eddie," he said.

"Hey."

"Did you call before?" he asked.

"No." My heart was pounding hard.

"Somebody called my house. Twice. They hung up both times."

"Yeah?"

"Yeah. If I ever find out who it is, I'm gonna beat him up," he growled. "I'll bet it was Kenny, trying to get back at me. He's probably gonna call you next."

"Yeah. Maybe."

"What do you wanna talk about?"

"Uhhhh," I was stalling. "I, uh, I thought you caught great today."

"Yeah?"

"Yeah. And I wanted to tell you."

"Thanks, Eddie," he said, sounding really happy. "I thought you threw great, too."

"When we play Kirby Carpenter he's not gonna have a chance," I said.

"If we play like we did today, he's history!" Bobby agreed.

I tried to think of something else to say, but my brain was still numb from talking to Jackie, so I said, "That's all I wanted to tell you."

After I hung up, I went back to my room feeling like I had thrown a winning touchdown. And I hoped more than anything that I would throw another one real soon.

Chapter Five

PERSONAL FOUL

It's really crazy how fast things can change. When I was watching the Jets game on Sunday, all I could think about was my dad and if he would make up with my mom and come back home. But after seeing Jackie, I could only think about her.

Everywhere I looked I saw Jackie.

The next morning, walking to school, when I looked up at the sun—I saw Jackie.

When I looked at the stop sign on the corner—I saw Jackie.

Everywhere I turned it was Jackie, Jackie, Jackie.

And when I headed into the schoolyard, I saw her for real, jumping rope with a few of her friends.

As I stood there watching her, I noticed that she didn't jump rope like the other girls. Most of them screamed as they jumped, so everybody had to notice what they were doing. But Jackie jumped in silence, a faint grin like a kitten's across her face. She bent her knees and her legs went up-down, up-down, up-down. She didn't say a word as her two friends whipped the jump ropes back and forth close to the ground. And my head went up-down, up-down, up-down, too, following Jackie's every movement.

I was startled out of staring by a familiar voice. "Hey, Eddie. What's up?"

"Nothing much," I said, turning toward Bobby, who was wearing a smile that looked a lot like his sister's.

"Guess who I just saw?" he asked.

"Who?"

"Kenny. And guess what he was doing?"

"Playing with his computer."

"Yeah. Wow," Bobby said, his smile vanishing. "How'd you guess?"

"Just lucky."

"But when he looked up at me, I gave him a real stare," Bobby said, shooting me his mean look. "If I ever catch him calling me and hanging up again, I'm gonna hurt him."

"Yeah?"

"Yeah. First, it's hanging up the phone. Next, he'll be coming over ringing my bell. I gotta watch out for my mom and my sister."

"I don't think he'll ring your bell," I said. "He's not like that."

"Anything new with your dad?" Bobby asked, taking me by surprise.

"No," I sighed, not wanting to admit that he still hadn't come home for good.

"That stinks," Bobby said.

"I think he might come home next weekend."

"My dad said he would come back," Bobby replied.

I said nothing.

"I'm going to the library after school. You wanna come with me?" Bobby asked.

"I don't know. What are you going for?"

"To start work on my science project. Gotta look up rocks."

"I gotta look up worms."

"Then come with me after school. We'll have fun."

Fun or not, the idea of Bobby spending the afternoon in the library, and Jackie possibly being home by herself interested me. I didn't want Bobby to become suspicious, so I didn't want to say "no" right away. Luckily I didn't have to, because the monitor blew her whistle, and we all had to line up.

When I got to our spot, there was the usual pushing and shoving until the monitor came near. Then everybody got into line. I looked to the left, two classes over, trying to see Jackie. But, as I was one of the shorter boys in my class, and as my line-mate was Daphne Slusarski, who had shot up so much in the past year she was sure to play center on the girls' basketball team once we got to junior high, it was pretty much impossible. Bobby was behind me, so I didn't want to stretch or jump up and down. I just kept turning slightly left every few seconds in hopes that Daphne would sneeze or double over with a throbbing pain. Then from the back of the line, I heard a voice that made my blood heat up. It was Kirby Carpenter, and he whispered one word:

"Giants."

"Yeahhhh," his teammate Sammy Green murmured.

I wanted to say, "Giants suck," but I knew Kirby was trying to get to me. So I kept looking forward and said nothing.

"On Sunday it's the Giants against the Lions," Kirby whispered. "Gonna destroy them more than any team has destroyed another in the history of the NFL."

Feeling like I was going to explode, I kept looking forward, but I couldn't help whispering one word:

"Jets."

"Yeahhhh," Bobby whispered in reply.

"This week it's the Jets against the Colts—" I went on.

But before I could finish my sentence, I heard, "Jets suck."

"Do not," I snapped back, straining to keep staring ahead.

"Lost two in a row, even with a new quarterback," Kirby said with a laugh.

"Not gonna lose this week," I replied, wanting to turn around and shoot laser beams out of my eyes right at him.

"Some teams are so sucky they need new quarterbacks,"

Kirby kept at me. "Just like some kids need new fathers."

That was all I could take.

"What did you say?" I demanded, spinning around.

"Don't worry. Your mom's probably got you a new dad already."

I don't remember much after that, except that I sprang at Kirby like a tiger that hadn't eaten in a week. My fists were clenched so tight that it felt like my fingers were welded together. I remember hitting him with my right, and then my left. We fell into a pile on the ground, tearing at each other's faces, as all the other kids crowded around and cheered and screamed. At some point, Kirby got his arms around my head. Then I saw the cement coming toward me at bullet speed. The next thing I remember was seeing my mother throwing open the door of the nurse's office and rushing in.

"Are you okay?" she demanded, zooming toward me.

"I think so," I groaned.

"He took a shot to the head. You should probably take him to the doctor," the nurse recommended.

That's just what my mom did. The doctor at the ER examined me and said my X-rays showed I didn't have a concussion. He said he didn't think I even needed an MRI. I went home with an icepack on my head and orders to take it easy.

This news made my mom relax a lot. But when we got home from the hospital, the principal of my school called, and Mom got upset all over again. This time she wasn't scared, though. She was furious. From my bedroom I could hear her arguing on the phone in the kitchen.

When the arguing stopped, I heard stomp-stomp footsteps on the stairs.

"I just got off the phone with your principal," she said as she stood in the doorway.

"Yeah?" I asked, lifting my throbbing head from my pillow.

"She's suspending you."

"What?!" I cried.

"She said you started the fight with Kirby."

"That's not true," I insisted.

"She said everybody said you punched first."

"He was talking about the Giants."

"That's no reason to start a fight."

"I was standing up to him," I said, sure she would appreciate my courage.

"Defending the Jets?"

"No."

"Admit it, Eddie. All you care about is football," she said, her eyes filled with anger.

"I don't care just about football."

"You eat, drink, sleep, and breathe football," she erupted. "If you were as responsible about your schoolwork as you are crazy about football, you'd be a genius. But to fight about it, especially with someone as big as Kirby, is really stupid."

"I didn't fight about football."

"What did you fight about then?"

"You."

"Huh?" She stopped cold.

"I fought with Kirby about you."

I hadn't wanted to tell her. I knew saying anything about my dad and her would make her upset, but I didn't seem to have a choice.

"Kirby Carpenter said something about me?" she asked.

"Yeah."

"What?"

"Nothing. It was nothing, Mom."

"Tell me, Eddie," she insisted.

I took a deep breath.

"He said I needed a whole new father . . . And that you had probably gotten me one already."

"Little brat," my mom snapped. "I should call his mother."

"Don't."

"She should know what her son is saying to people."

"I'm gonna take care of Kirby. I'm gonna beat him."

"At football, you mean?" she asked.

"Yeah. At football."

Mom just stood there, shaking her head. "When I met your father, all he wanted to do was play football. You're turning out just like him."

"What's wrong with that?" I asked.

Then my mother's face fell, and she suddenly looked very sad.

"Nothing," she finally said, after a long moment.

"I'm gonna beat him, Mom," I said, trying to sound confident enough for both of us.

"Maybe you will," my mom said softly. "Just don't get into fights. I don't want you getting hurt."

"How long am I suspended for?"

"Just tomorrow."

"You didn't want me to go to school anyway," I said and tried to force a smile. It hurt.

For the rest of the day I lay in bed, trying to think up new plays that would completely humiliate Kirby Carpenter. But as my headache slowly disappeared, I thought less and less about Kirby, and more and more about Jackie. I knew she had seen the fight. Everybody in the schoolyard had. I wondered if she had cheered me on. She couldn't possibly have cheered for Kirby. Then I worried that she might hate fighting and think that I was a jerk for trying to punch somebody out. Lots of girls were like that. Especially smart girls. And Jackie Rodriguez was definitely a smart girl.

I worried so much about what Jackie thought about me that I couldn't lie still anymore. So I decided I would somehow have to make it to my mom's room and call her. But then I heard footsteps again. Thankfully, these were pat-pat footsteps. Then my mom appeared in the doorway.

"How are you feeling?" she asked.

"My headache went away."

"I have to go to the store. Will you be okay if I leave you for a half-hour?"

"Sure."

When I heard the car vrooming into the distance, I threw off my covers, got out of bed, and headed down the hall. But then I remembered that Bobby was spending the afternoon at the library looking up rocks. I stood there completely still and then decided to do what any quarterback would do when an opportunity presented itself: I'd go for it all.

Mom would only be gone for half an hour, which meant that I had to get a lot done in a short period of time. It would be:

Me: "Hi, is Bobby home?"

Jackie: "He's not here."

Me: "Oh, yeah, I forgot he was going to the library."

Then I'd find out if she thought I was a jerk, and leave.

When I got to Bobby's house, I took a deep breath, headed up to the door, and pressed the bell. Before I could exhale, Jackie answered the door—and I became completely paralyzed. She looked so . . . amazing. Her hair hung loose to her shoulders, and she was wearing a plain white T-shirt and cut-off jeans, with nothing on her tiny feet.

"Hi, Eddie," she said, looking surprised that I was standing there.

I tried to say, "Hi, Jackie," but what came out sounded more like what you hear on TV when somebody's been kidnapped, tied up, and has tape over his mouth. "Mmmmmm."

"Bobby's not here. He went to the library," she continued.

"Mmmmm, mmmmm," I mumbled.

"How are you feeling?" she asked.

I gave her a long reply, "Mmmmm, mmmmm, mmmmm, mmmmm."

"You're lucky you didn't get a concussion," she said. Then I realized that I had to be making sense or she wouldn't have answered me.

A minute later we were sitting on her couch, and she was giving me apple juice and chocolate chip cookies.

"Does your head hurt?" she asked, looking concerned.

"It did. But it doesn't anymore," I assured her.

"Your doctor should have sent you for an MRI," she said.

"He said I didn't need one."

"Well, if I was your doctor, I would have sent you for an MRI. Then you'd know if there was any serious damage." She continued, "I saw Kirby push your head into the ground. It looked horrible."

"It felt horrible, too."

"I heard you guys were fighting about football."

"No," I protested. "It started that way. But then he said something . . . something about my mom."

"That's terrible. If somebody said something mean about my mom, I might hit him, too."

I nodded quickly. She was starting to see things my way.

"But Kirby's so big," she went on. "You were heroic."

All of a sudden I felt completely relieved. I wasn't a jerk. I was "heroic."

"You're oozing," she said, pointing to the patch on my forehead.

I touched it with my finger, and it felt all wet.

"Yech," I said.

"Don't touch it. I'll fix it."

She led me to the bathroom, sat me down, took off my bandage, and placed a washcloth on my wound.

"Owww."

"Come on. It doesn't hurt that much," she teased.

"It does."

"It doesn't look so bad," she said, smiling.

She looked straight into my eyes, and the pain started to go away.

After she finished putting on a new bandage, we went back downstairs to finish the cookies. Bobby burst through the door carrying a stack of library books.

"Hey. Eddie. How are you feeling?" he said. He put down the books and rushed over to look closely at my injury.

"Pretty good," I smiled.

"I thought you would be in the hospital or something."

"It was just a cut. Jackie changed the bandage for me."

"You really gave it to him, man," Bobby said, his face tightening up. "He'll probably be out of school for a week."

"He insulted my mom. Nobody gets away with that."

"No kidding," he said. Then he stopped, and with a confused look, he asked, "What are you doing here, anyway?"

"I came to get the homework," I said without missing a beat.

"I told you I was going to the library."

"I forgot. I hit my head. Remember?"

"Wow. Yeah," Bobby said.

Mrs. Rodriguez called Jackie into the kitchen to help her with dinner. Bobby gave me the homework, and I told him that while I was lying in bed, I had thought up a new play that would make Kirby's defense look like a joke.

"What is it?" he asked.

"A double hook slant."

"Wow. Do you wanna show it to me?"

I knew that I shouldn't throw a football right then. But I also knew that all the great quarterbacks played injured. Bobby grabbed his football, and we headed into the street.

"Sean and Marty will run ten yards on both sides of me," I said, as I drew the play with my finger on my hand. "Then they'll hook, and you'll slant from right to left."

"Wow. Great play!"

I took the ball and dropped back, as Bobby ran just where I'd showed him to run. I threw it hard. The catch was never in doubt.

We practiced the play four more times, until the front door opened and Mrs. Rodriguez came out.

"Eddie. Your mom was just on the phone," she called to me. "She wants you home right now."

Crap, I thought, sure that I was really going to be in trouble now. But it didn't really matter to me.

Because Jackie Rodriguez thought I was a hero.

Chapter Six

A HAIL MARY

When I got home from Bobby's, my mother was furious.

"I thought I told you to stay in bed!" she screamed at me. "But you had to go over to Bobby's to play football!"

I wanted to tell her that football had nothing to do with it. But since I couldn't tell her the real reason I went over to Bobby's, I just nodded and looked at the ground.

"You hurt your head this morning. And now you take another risk. That's crazy," she went on. "You're grounded for a week."

I didn't argue with her.

I kept a low profile all week and felt better each day. Finally, I got my team together for practice. The week off showed, and Marty and Sean were up to their old tricks of dropping balls and tripping over clumps of dead grass.

"It's okay, guys," I said, sounding as optimistic as possible. "We'll get it together."

And with each practice they did get a little better. Or at least I convinced myself they did.

The situation at home didn't get much better, though.

Dad came over on Sunday to watch the Jets play the Bengals.

"Hey, Mister," he called as he came through the door.

"Hey, Dad," I muttered.

"I heard you took a hit," he said, glancing at my forehead. "You look okay."

"He's lucky," Mom said. "It could have been really bad. You should have been here, Tommy."

"I had to work," my father snapped. "Let's not. Okay?"

"No. Let's not say anything meaningful. Let's just watch the game and eat, like always," my mom said. She turned on the TV and headed into the kitchen.

The game was bad for the Jets. Their offense just couldn't get going. At first my dad didn't say much, and neither did I. It was like we weren't in the same room. But then he relaxed and started smiling and talking about football and the work he was doing at the shop. I wanted to have fun with him. I wanted to believe everything was really all right. But I couldn't. I just sat there, watching the Jets make bad play after bad play, finally going down in defeat, 34-10.

After the game ended, my mom served dinner. We all sat down and dug in, and my dad kept talking and smiling, not noticing that no one else was saying much. When the table was cleared and the dishes were washed, Dad gave me a hug and said, "See you soon, Mister." Then he headed toward the door.

"You're leaving?" my mom asked.

"Pretty much," he replied.

"If you leave this time, Tommy, don't come back."

My body went ice-cold. I looked up at my mom. She looked more serious than I had ever seen her.

"Jeanie—" he started.

"Look around! Look at what you're giving up. You can't come and go as you please. You can't treat this home like a restaurant and us like the workers."

"You don't understand."

"You're right. I don't," she said. "I tried. But I just don't. You have to make a decision."

My dad looked at each of us. Took a good long look. Then he swallowed hard, turned, and left.

As his car pulled away, my mom slumped onto the couch. I slumped down next to her. We didn't say a word.

Eventually I headed upstairs. I tried to fall asleep, but I was too sad to sleep. Even too sad to cry anymore. After a while, my head started to hurt. I decided to get some Tylenol, and as I headed into the hall, I heard two voices coming from the kitchen. Was Dad back? I listened closer. One voice definitely belonged to my mom—but the other voice was my Aunt Lori's.

"I just don't know what to do, Lori," my mom said. "I feel like everything is coming apart, and I can't stop it."

"I wish I could give you some advice," Aunt Lori replied.

"Just being here is helpful. Thanks for coming over," Mom said.

Trying to be as quiet as possible, I tiptoed to the landing so I could hear them a little better.

"Does he say anything about coming home?" Mom asked.

"No. He doesn't say much about anything," Aunt Lori replied. "Joey tries to get him talking, but he just sits on the porch looking out into the distance. Joey would like him to come back to you. It's not that we have a space problem, but we'd like to have a little time to ourselves."

"I knew he wasn't exactly happy," my mom said, "but—"

"But nothing," Aunt Lori interrupted. "It's out of your control. When men get to a certain age, they get a little crazy. Especially if they think they haven't done something big."

I moved my foot a little, and the floor squeaked. Before I could even turn, my mom stuck her head out of the kitchen doorway and saw me standing on the landing.

"What are you doing there?" she demanded.

"Nothing," I stammered.

"Were you listening to what we were saying?"

"No."

"Tell me the truth," she demanded, her face turning red. "Were you listening to us?"

"I was getting something for my headache."

"Then why are you on the landing?"

"Because I heard you."

My mom's eyes turned radioactive. "Get to your room right now!"

I turned, ran back into my room, and closed the door so hard that my window rattled.

As I lay there in the silent room, I thought about what I'd heard Aunt Lori say. My father hadn't come home because he hadn't done anything big. But what big things did he want to do? He didn't want to be President of the United States or Governor of New Jersey. All I could think of was the times he told me that when he was a kid he had wanted to be quarterback of the Jets. But he wasn't even good enough to play first-string safety in high school. Okay, that must have felt lousy. But that was a really long time ago. Almost forever. He couldn't still be thinking about that.

I heard footsteps heading my way. My whole body tightened up. Then my door opened and Mom stood there, her mouth drooping at the sides, her eyes looking as if she hadn't slept for days. As soon as I saw her, I knew she wasn't going to yell at me. In fact, she didn't say anything. She just stood there looking, and looking, and looking. Finally she spoke. "You shouldn't have been eavesdropping on me."

"I know."

"How am I supposed to trust you if I think you're listening in on my conversations?"

"I wasn't trying to. I didn't even know Aunt Lori was here," I said, defending myself. "I opened my door, and then I heard her."

"You shouldn't have listened to our conversation."

I nodded.

"But I shouldn't have yelled at you," she went on. "I didn't mean to. It just came out. Did you do your homework?"

"Most of it," I told her. "I still have reading to do."

"Well, finish up. Then get ready for bed."

I nodded again.

"Give me a hug," she said, opening her arms to me.

I really needed a hug right then. We put our arms around each other, and it felt really good.

When I went to school the next day, I didn't see Bobby in the schoolyard. As soon as I sat down in class, Ms. Gregg announced that Bobby would be absent. I groaned so loud that the entire class turned toward me. I was sorry that he wasn't feeling well, but I was even sorrier that he wouldn't be at practice. In fact, the thought of practice without Bobby was so horrible that at lunch I told Sean and Marty that we'd postpone it a day and see if he made it to school tomorrow. They didn't seem to mind. Then I spoke with Jackie.

"How's he doing?" I asked.

"Not good. Last night he had a sore throat. Then he started sneezing," she told me.

"Do you think he'll be in school tomorrow?"

"I don't think so. I told him to take Tylenol because he was running a temperature. My mom is gonna take him to the doctor. I'm pretty sure he'll give Bobby an antibiotic. Maybe amoxicillin. Or Zithromax. Either one would work just fine."

Looking into Jackie's eyes, I had an idea. It hit me as hard as a defensive tackle hits a quarterback on third-and-goal from the five.

"We were gonna practice today," I told her. "Then we were gonna go for pizza. Just Bobby and me. But I guess that's not gonna happen . . ."

Then I sucked in a chest full of air, and tried to keep the hamburger I had just eaten from making a return trip to the light of day.

". . . Unless you'd like to have pizza with me?"

"Me?" Jackie asked, sounding pretty surprised.

"Yeah. It's no fun having pizza alone," I said, trying to smile.

Jackie giggled.

And I waited.

She giggled again.

And I waited a little more.

Finally, she said, "Sure."

I felt like jumping around the schoolyard. But I didn't. I just held it all in and said, "Great. See you after school." Then I stumbled to the far end of the yard, just to feel good by myself about winning a big one. The Jackie Bowl. Which right then seemed bigger than any playoff game or Super Bowl I could possibly imagine.

I met Jackie after school, and we walked up Elwell Road to Louie's Pizza. Lucky for me it was Monday, and I still had most of my allowance. We each ordered a couple of slices and sat down at one of the round tables.

"I'm really sorry Bobby's sick," I said, nervously biting off the tip of one pizza slice. "Tell him he's got to get better real soon so we can practice. I don't want to practice without him."

"I'll tell him," Jackie said.

For a long moment I chewed and chewed and chewed, trying to think of something to say. Finally, I came up with something that didn't sound too lame. "He's really lucky to have you for a sister."

"You think so?"

"You fix his cuts. You give him Tylenol."

"If Bobby listened to me, he wouldn't be sick," she said, looking straight at me, her brown eyes shining. "He doesn't wash his hands enough. I tell him, germs travel on your hands. But his hands are always dirty. And he's always putting his fingers in his mouth."

"You think that's how he got sick?" I asked.

"Probably," she said.

"I usually wash my hands. All the time," I lied.

"I thought so," she said and smiled. "That's why you're not sick, and my brother is."

We talked about school—her favorite subjects, my favorite subjects, her parents, and finally mine.

"How are your mom and dad doing?" she asked me.

"I guess everybody knows," I sighed.

"Kinda."

"They're okay," I said, tensing up a little. "My dad came over yesterday. We watched the Jets game."

"They lost."

"I asked Bobby what it was like when your dad left. He said he didn't remember your dad."

Jackie looked down at the table, then said, "I remember my dad. Bobby does, too. It was bad."

"I'm sorry," I said, wishing I hadn't brought up the subject.

"We thought he was going to come back. But he didn't. I cried a lot. Bobby cried even more."

"I'm really sorry."

"It's okay," she said, looking at me again. "I hope your dad comes back."

"He will," I said. "Everything's gonna be okay."

"Good," she said, nodding.

We finished our drinks, threw away our garbage, and left the pizzeria. The sky was darkening, and the wind was tearing the last leaves from the trees, blowing them in circles just above the ground.

"It's late. I'd better hurry," Jackie said, looking anxiously at the stormy sky.

"I'll walk you."

"It's okay."

"At least to your block," I said, thinking she might not want her mom or her brother to see me walking her home.

"Okay," she agreed.

When we got to Eldridge Street, we stopped and looked straight into each other's eyes. I had looked at Jackie a lot of times over the past few weeks, but I had never stood so close to her.

Finally, after looking at her as long as I could without blinking, I said, "Thank you."

She broke into a smile.

"Maybe we could have pizza again sometime?" I asked her.

"Sure," she nodded.

"Maybe tomorrow?"

And she agreed.

Jackie and I had pizza together the next day, the day after that, and the day after that. On Tuesday she ordered a slice with broccoli on it, because she said vegetables were good for a person's diet. On Wednesday she had garlic knots instead of pizza, because too much cheese was bad for the digestive system. She said if I didn't believe her, I could look it up on the Internet. She even gave me the name of the Web site. I didn't care about my digestive system, but I downed a slice with olives and onions to show her I knew how to eat healthy.

When we sat down at our table on Thursday, she said something I really didn't want to hear. "Bobby's feeling a lot better," she told me. "I think he'll be in school tomorrow."

"Oh. Great," I said, trying to sound happy.

"I knew an antibiotic would make him well."

"You're gonna be a great doctor, Jackie."

"Did you look up that Web site I told you about?"

"Uhhh . . ." I started to say.

"You didn't," she said, her smile turning into a smirk.

"Not yet. But I'm gonna."

"You should keep up on science, Eddie. You're too smart to not know what's going on."

"Me? Smart?" I asked. "You're the one in the gifted class."

"So what? It doesn't matter what class you're in. You're

very smart. I've always thought so."

I replayed in my head the three words Jackie said to me: "You're very smart." I started to feel warm, like I did when my dad and mom took me to the shore last summer, and the sun was way up in the sky, and the sand was soft, and everything seemed just right.

When we left Louie's Pizza, the sun was just beginning to fade into the distance, and the wind was just starting to cut through the bare tree branches. I walked Jackie to her block, talking all the way about my science project on worms, but thinking about how our time was running out. When we got to her block, my hands were shaking and my entire body was tingling from head to toe. I turned and looked right at her.

"J-J-Jackie?" I stammered.

"Yes?" she said, looking right back at me, suddenly seeming almost as nervous as I was.

I tried to speak, but my throat was too tight.

I tried again.

Then again.

Finally, I managed to squeeze out a sentence.

"Can I . . . have your e-mail address?"

"My e-mail address?" she said, looking surprised.

"Yeah. May I have it?"

"Sure," she said, then pulled a piece of paper from her book bag, scribbled the address on it, and handed it to me.

"Great. I'll e-mail you," I said, folding the paper and jamming it into my pocket.

Part of me wanted to turn and run. But the other part of me knew the clock was ticking. So I threw a Hail Mary.

"J-Jackie?" I stammered once again.

"Yes?" she said, nervous like before.

Again, I managed to squeeze out a sentence.

"May I . . . kiss you?"

I waited for the rejection. I wanted for her to laugh, or cry, or run screaming up the street. But she didn't do any of those things. She just kept looking at me and said a soft, simple, "Yes."

Then I pressed my lips to hers and felt a sensation that was so powerful, so amazing, so overwhelming that for one moment everything stopped. Everything. And Jackie and I were the only two people who mattered anywhere in the universe.

I don't remember much about my walk home. I don't remember if I met anybody, or talked to anybody, or if it rained, or snowed, or if a UFO landed and asked me directions to Washington, D.C. I do know that I felt incredible—and more peaceful than I had felt in a really long time.

When I got home, the house was shaking with the roar of my mom vacuuming.

"How was practice?" she asked, turning off the vacuum.

"Ummm. Okay," I answered.

She looked puzzled and asked, "Are you all right?"

"Why?" I asked back, getting a little nervous.

"You look a little flushed. Are you feeling okay?"

"I'm great. You wouldn't believe how great I am."

Mom wrinkled her forehead with a puzzled look, but I just headed upstairs, fell backwards on my bed, looked up at the ceiling, and smiled.

Chapter Seven

OUT OF BOUNDS

Just like Jackie said, Bobby showed up at school the next day. And we began practicing again. But through all of our practices, I kept thinking of Jackie. Although I didn't include her in anything Bobby and I did, I tried my best to keep contact with her in ways other kids wouldn't notice.

In the schoolyard I looked hard at her whenever she was playing with her friends, hoping that she would feel my stare and turn to look at me. Sometimes she did, and she always smiled at me. But her smile was just big enough for me and only me to see. It was our secret, and it made me feel so amazing.

In the lunchroom I sometimes shot a look over toward her table while Bobby kept talking to me about football or homework or how he was gonna get Kenny Blatt.

One time Bobby caught me.

"What are you looking at?" he asked, turning in Jackie's direction.

I grabbed him by the top of his head and spun him back toward me.

"Don't look!" I yelled.

"Ow!"

"Don't look," I insisted. "It's Kirby."

"Yeah. Wow," he said. "But don't grab my head. That hurt."

The best was when I'd see Jackie get up to go to the bathroom during lunch. I would wait a minute, and then get up, too. If I timed it right (and I usually did), I got to the boys' bathroom just as she was coming out of the girls' bathroom. She would smile, say a quick "hi," and I would do the same. Then she would head back to her table, and I would head into the boys' room as if nothing special had happened.

Did other kids see us? Sure.

Did they know what we were doing? Maybe.

But it never got back to Bobby. And that's what mattered.

Things were happening with the team, too. Sean and Marty had improved a lot. Bobby was catching everything I threw at him. And I was throwing longer than I ever had. So we decided it was time to take on Kirby Carpenter.

Fixing a date to play was difficult. I didn't want to speak to Kirby. Just looking at him made my temperature skyrocket. Every day, as I sat across from him in class, I'd want to get up and push my right fist through his nose and out the other side of his head. But I knew I couldn't do it. I had been suspended once. A second suspension might stop me from going to junior high. So I held it all in, deciding I would get my revenge as I had always wanted—on the football field. I sent Bobby to talk with him about a game. Less than a minute later, Bobby came back to where Marty, Sean, and I were standing in the corner of the schoolyard and said, "He won't talk to me."

"What?" I said.

"He'll only talk to you."

The last thing I wanted to do was talk to Kirby. I would rather have to do research in a worm swamp than talk to Kirby. But when I looked at the sad faces of Bobby, Sean, and Marty, I knew I had to talk to him. Besides, I wanted to play him like nothing else in the world—except kiss Jackie again. So I fixed a stern quarterback look on my face and headed over to where Kirby was standing with his obnoxious teammates. Bobby, Sean, and Marty followed me at a safe distance.

"Hey, Paulsen. What are you doing in my section of the yard?" Kirby said as he sneered down at me.

"Heard you wanted to talk to me," I said.

"Heard you wanted to talk to me," he replied.

I held my breath and said, "We want to set up a game."

"Yeah? Well, don't waste your breath. I'm not gonna play you."

"What?!" I yelled.

"You insulted me."

"You insulted me. And you also insulted my mom."

"You wanna play me, you gotta apologize."

"No way I'm gonna apologize to you."

I snapped my head around to start walking away. Bobby, Sean, and Marty couldn't have looked sadder if their dogs had died. I knew I couldn't let them down. And I knew that I wanted to play Kirby so bad, so I could beat him so bad, worse than he'd ever been beaten. I clenched my teeth like I do when the doctor gives me a shot and let out a tight, "I apologize."

"How much?" Kirby demanded.

"What?"

"How much do you apologize?"

I clenched my teeth harder and squeaked, "A lot."

"How much 'a lot'?"

"What do you mean 'how much a lot'?" I said, wanting to pound him to the ground, suspension or not.

"I mean, how much a lot do you apologize?"

"A lot, a lot," I snapped. "I apologize more than I ever apologized ever."

Kirby stood there silently for a moment. Then he said, "I'll think about it."

"You'll think about it?!" I screamed, lurching toward him. My teammates rushed up to hold me back.

"Yeah. I'll think about it, moron," he said, pushing me in the chest.

"There's nothing to think about. I apologized. You have to play."

"I don't have to do nothing."

"You're just scared. You know I have a new team, and that we've been practicing, and that we can probably beat you."

"You can't beat me."

"Prove it. Play us."

"I'll play you. I'll play any team you want," he finally let loose. "Even the real Jets. They stink just like you do."

"Saturday?" I asked, sure he wouldn't turn me down.

"Saturday. Same as usual," he agreed.

Then the monitor blew her whistle, and everybody started lining up. But before we headed to our lines, I turned to my teammates, made a fist, and raised it triumphantly into the air.

I came out of school that afternoon feeling like I'd been voted MVP because of my agreement with Kirby. Bobby walked along with me, as usual. Then I saw somebody standing at the curb next to an old blue Chevy. That somebody was my dad. All of the good feelings inside me disappeared like water down an open drain.

"Hey, Mister," he called over.

"Hey, Dad," I said back, weakly. I turned toward Bobby and said, "See you tomorrow."

"You sure you wanna talk to him?" Bobby asked protectively.

"It's okay," I said, and started to walk over to where my father was standing.

"How're you doing?" he asked, smiling down at me and poking me in the shoulder.

"Okay. What are you doing here?"

"I was driving by, and I saw everybody coming out. I thought I'd drive you home."

"Oh. Great," I said, trying to smile back at him.

"Jump in."

And I did. Then he pulled away from the curb and drove up Elwell Road.

"How was school today?" he asked, his eyes focused on the traffic.

"Good," I told him, hoping that he really wanted to know how things were.

"Do anything interesting?"

"A report on worms."

"Worms. Yech. The only thing a worm is good for is to bait a hook."

"Yeah," I agreed, starting to relax a little.

After saying nothing for a few moments, he asked, "How's your mom?"

"Okay," I replied, tensing up again.

"Just okay?"

"She's good. But she's looking for a new job. Full-time hours."

"I know. It's not easy. She's a strong woman. Be good to her."

I wanted to tell him that I thought he should be good to her. But I didn't say a thing. I just sat there in silence, waiting for him to say something important about something important, like I'd waited when he came over each Sunday to watch football. But, as usual, he said nothing. And by the time we got home, I felt like a jerk, because once again I thought he might come through. But he didn't. He never came through anymore, and probably never would no matter how hard I hoped.

"I have something for you," he said as we got out of the car.

"What?"

"Come here," he said, moving toward the trunk. He then opened it and revealed a brand-new, Brooks-Bollinger-edition pro football.

"Wow!" I cried.

"Take it," he said, smiling bigger than he had in a long time. "They just got it into the stores. When I saw it, I knew I had to get you one."

"Thanks, Dad," I said, carefully taking it into my hands.

"That's a football that wins games," he declared.

"We're gonna play Kirby on Saturday," I said, the words pouring out. "We're gonna beat him bad."

"Play with that football and you can't lose."

Then I heard a thump. I looked up, and he was back in the car, his door shut tight.

"You're leaving?" I asked.

"Gotta get back to the shop," he said through the open window. "You should come down someday. Working on a '66 Corvette. A real beauty."

He gave me another poke in the shoulder and drove away, leaving me alone on the curb with my books and my new football.

When my mom came home, I told her that Dad had picked me up from school.

"Really?" she asked. "Did you know he was going to pick you up?"

"No. It was a surprise," I said.

"He gave you that football?"

"Yeah. It's great."

Mom stared at the football as if it were some kind of space-alien baby that I'd found on the street.

"It's very nice," she finally said and silently walked away.

The ball felt heavy in my hands. My dad said he had stopped by school because he saw kids coming out. But if he had the football in his trunk, then what he said was a lie. The football was more like a bribe than a present. But it didn't make me like him any more than I had. In fact, after seeing Mom walk away from me, I liked him even less. So I put it on the floor and looked at it for a long time. It looked so much nicer than my dirty, cut-up football. Nicer than any football I had ever seen. But I decided that I didn't want to play with it. So I took it upstairs to my room, threw it into my closet, and hoped that by the next time I opened the closet door, it would have magically disappeared.

We had only five short days to get ready for the game, so we agreed to practice every day. Monday afternoon we got together in the park. Right away things went badly. Marty kept forgetting the plays. Sean limped the whole time because his new sneakers had given him a blister. And I threw . . . well, lousy. I don't know why. The week before I had thrown great. But now that the game was set, my arm had no strength, and my passes had no zip.

"What's the matter, Eddie?" Bobby called after I under-threw a down-and-in, letting him hit the ground with nothing in his hands and dirt in his face.

"Sorry," I called back.

"If we play like this on Saturday, we're gonna get

creamed," he barked.

Then in the distance I saw something that made me stop cold. It was Mikey Mantello walking hand-in-hand with Dana McAllister. They were walking together for everybody to see. And right then I stopped thinking about football. I wanted to be Mikey. But I didn't want to be with Dana. I wanted to be with Jackie. I wanted to be with her more than I wanted to win any game. And I had a great idea.

"I don't think we should practice in the park anymore," I announced.

"Why not?" Bobby asked.

"Who says we're not being watched?" I said.

"Huh?" said Sean.

"Kirby is smart. He'll do anything to win a game. Who says he doesn't have some of his guys watching us right now?"

"I don't see anybody," Marty said, chewing a wad of bubble gum as he looked out at the open field.

"Not here. Behind those trees. Or over that hill," I replied, pointing way into the distance.

"Wow! That makes sense. He probably is spying on us," Bobby said. "That's probably why we always lose to him."

"We've gotta practice in private," I suggested.

"Where?" Sean asked.

"At our houses," I said. "Tomorrow we'll practice at Bobby's. Wednesday at Sean's. Thursday at Marty's. And

Friday at mine. Okay?"

"Okay," they all agreed.

The next day we met at Bobby's to practice in total secrecy.

First, I started with screen passes to both sides.

Next, I threw bullets over the middle.

Then, I moved onto my special double-hook slant.

Every few minutes I shot a look toward Bobby's house to see if I could spot Jackie. Most times I saw nothing. But a few times I glimpsed her. Once I saw her walk past the front window. Then I saw her profile in an upstairs window. But I didn't smile, wave, or do anything to attract anybody's attention. I just threw harder and harder, hitting my receiver square-on every time, until all four of us were bushed, and we had to have drinks. We followed Bobby into the house.

"Mom, can we have some soda?" he called.

"Soda. Soda. Everybody wants soda," Mrs. Rodriguez chimed.

"We've been playing hard," Bobby told her.

"Make sure you wipe your feet," she instructed him.

As Bobby led Sean and Marty into the kitchen, I excused myself to go to the bathroom. I climbed the stairs, my heart pounding and my palms sweating. But instead of going to the bathroom, I walked down the hall to Jackie's room.

She looked up from her desk and saw me standing in the doorway. "Hey," she said, sounding surprised.

"Hey," I whispered back. "Can I come in?"

"Sure."

I stepped lightly into her room, trying hard not to make one board creak.

"What are you doing?" I asked.

"Homework."

"On what?"

"How the human ear works."

"I never do my homework till after dinner."

"I like to get to it right away. I guess I'm weird," she said.

"Did you watch us practice?" I asked.

"A little," she said, lowering her eyes.

"How'd we look?"

"Really good. I think you're gonna win."

I stopped thinking. Something took hold of me and moved me straight toward her. When I reached her desk, she stood up, and I moved my mouth toward her mouth and placed my lips against her lips. And it was great. But in the deepest part of my brain, I sensed that something was wrong. Then I heard Bobby's voice.

"What are you doing?"

Jackie and I froze. Then we moved apart really fast.

"What are you doing?" he repeated.

We both turned toward him. He didn't look happy.

"What-are-you-doing?" he asked again.

I tried to think of an answer he might believe. But all I could come up with was, "Nothing."

"You were kissing her," he accused.

"N-n-no," I stammered.

"You were kissing my sister."

"Okay. I was," I admitted, starting to shake.

"Why were you kissing my sister?"

"Bobby—" Jackie began to say.

But he snapped a quick "be quiet!" at her and turned back to me. "Why were you kissing my sister?"

I looked into his eyes and saw a fire I'd never seen in Bobby before. I decided to come clean and said, "Because I like her."

"You can't like her!"

"Bobby—" Jackie tried again.

"You can't like my sister! She'll like you back, and then you'll have a fight, and then she'll get upset, and everything will be terrible again. Get out!"

"Bobby—"

"Get outta here!"

"Bobby—" Jackie pleaded.

"Be quiet!" he yelled at her. Then he grabbed me by the arm and yanked me from her room and toward the stairs, shouting, "Get out!" over and over again.

"What's going on?" Sean called from below.

"Bobby, what's the matter?" Mrs. Rodriguez demanded.

"He was kissing Jackie!" Bobby cried, shoving me down the stairs.

"Bobby—" I said, grabbing onto the railing so I wouldn't fall.

"You can't kiss my sister!"

"Bobby, stop it!" his mother insisted.

"He can't kiss my sister! I won't let anybody kiss my sister!"

He shoved me hard in the chest. I flew off the bottom step, hung in the air for what seemed like forever, and finally crashed onto the floor.

"Bobby!" his mother shrieked.

"Get out!" Bobby yelled at me. "Get out! Get out!"

He pulled me up off the floor by the neck of my T-shirt as if I weighed barely a pound and pitched me toward the door.

Mrs. Rodriguez kept shouting for him to stop, and I could hear Jackie crying really loud behind us. But Bobby kept yelling at me and pushing me forward. Before I could say his name one more time, I found myself tripping down the front steps, soaring into the air once again, extending my arms to break my fall, and then sprawling onto the sidewalk, with Sean and Marty rushing out after me.

"I'm off the team! Forever!" Bobby shouted from the doorway. He slammed the door so hard the cement underneath me actually shook.

I stayed sprawled on the cement for a couple of minutes, dizzy and shaking. I could still hear Bobby and his mother yelling at each other and Jackie crying from inside the house. I wanted to go back inside and talk to her, but I was afraid that if I rang the bell, he would kill me. So I just lay there, weakly looking up at Marty and Sean, knowing that everything I had worked so hard to put together had just collapsed. And there was nothing I could do to fix it.

Chapter Eight

RUNNING BACK

I finally managed to lift myself off the cement and stagger away from Bobby's house. I wanted to say something to Sean and Marty, but couldn't think of anything that made any sense. I really wanted them to say something to me. But I guess they couldn't think of anything either, because they walked with me to the corner in stunned silence.

"He was really mad," Sean finally said.

"He was crazy," I corrected him.

"What are we gonna do?" Marty asked.

"I don't know. I'm outta here," I grunted and turned to start on my way home.

When I got home, my house was almost completely silent. Mom was sitting at the kitchen table, staring down at the help-wanted ads. I could smell dinner cooking in the oven.

"How was practice?" Mom asked, her face pale with sadness.

"Okay," I mumbled.

"I guess you're almost ready for the game," she went on.

"Okay," I answered automatically. Then I left the room

and headed upstairs.

As soon as I walked into my room, I heard the phone ring. I knew it was Mrs. Rodriguez. In a few seconds my mom would know everything, and I'd be grounded forever. Not that it would matter. Jackie wouldn't be able to see me anymore. And my team had broken up. What did I need free time for anyway?

It wasn't long before I heard Mom's footsteps on the stairs.

"Eddie, I just got a phone call," she said, stepping through my doorway.

I barely looked up.

"It was Mrs. Rodriguez," she continued. "She told me you and Bobby got into a fight."

I nodded.

"Do you want to tell me about it?" she asked.

I shrugged.

"Come on, Eddie. I want you to tell me."

"Was Mrs. Rodriguez upset?"

"A little. She said Bobby got very angry. She wanted to know if you were okay."

I shrugged again.

"She told me Bobby caught you kissing Jackie."

"Kinda," I mumbled, looking at the floor.

"Kinda?"

"Yeah. I kinda kissed Jackie," I admitted, peering up at her.

My mom sighed a big sigh, looked away, then looked right back at me. I thought she was going to get mad and really give it to me. But she didn't. She just asked, "Why did you kiss her?"

"Because I wanted to."

"Do you like her?"

I stopped for a second. I wanted to lie, but I knew that I couldn't.

"Yeah," I said. "I do."

"And Bobby got mad?"

"He went crazy. I thought he was gonna kill me."

"Jackie Rodriguez is a nice girl, Eddie, but you're both too young."

"I wasn't trying to hurt her."

"I know. But it's too soon. And I don't want you to get hurt."

"I'm not gonna get hurt."

Mom sighed and looked away for a second. "People don't always feel the way you think they feel."

"Like Dad?" I blurted out.

She stopped like I'd slapped her across the face.

"No," she finally said. "It's different with Dad."

"Did you talk to him?" I asked.

"No."

"Are you gonna call him?"

"No. He's the one who has to make the call."

She then turned and headed out of my room.

I didn't sleep very much that night. I kept thinking of Bobby screaming at me and pushing me down the stairs. I knew Bobby didn't want any guys going after his sister, but I went after her anyway and kissed her in his own house. Because of that I ruined the most important thing I'd ever wanted to do—beat Kirby Carpenter. Then I remembered what Aunt Lori had said: My dad was upset because he had never done anything important. I tried to do something that was important to me, and I failed. If Dad felt anything like I did, I knew he was feeling pretty lousy.

When I got up the next morning, I was still depressed.

"Aren't you going to eat anything?" my mom asked.

"I'm not hungry," I replied.

"Try to eat. Please," my mom said, pushing a plate of scrambled eggs closer to me.

"I'll try."

I tried. But I failed. Big time.

By the time I got to school, I decided I had to clear things up with Bobby. He was my best friend. I didn't want him to hate me forever. So even though I was still really nervous, I decided I would try to talk to him about what happened. I was sure he would have cooled down a little, especially if his mother had punished him. But when I saw him in the school-yard, and our eyes met, his face turned as cold and as hard as a cement wall. I watched him all morning in class, and he stayed the same way. He didn't eat lunch with me—the first time since we'd become friends. And when school ended, he marched straight out of class and headed home by himself.

I was standing on the curb, feeling pretty lousy again, when I saw Marty and Sean come out of the building. A gust of wind blew Marty's hat off. But he snapped out his hand and grabbed it before it hit the ground. If he only were that good with a football, I thought.

"What's up?" I asked them.

They both mumbled that they were okay, so I decided to get to the point.

"You guys get over yesterday?" I asked.

"Sort of," Sean said, looking nervously at the ground.

"I wanted to talk to Bobby today. But he still looked mad. I guess he's not gonna be on the team."

"We don't really have a team," Marty replied.

"There's still the three of us," I told him, trying to sound optimistic.

"What good's a team with only three players when Kirby

has four?" Sean asked.

"Not much. But if we could get a fourth—" I started.

"Who's gonna want to play with us?" Marty snapped.

"Whatta you mean?" I challenged.

"I mean, we're supposed to play Kirby on Saturday. Nobody's gonna wanna work that hard. Especially when we're gonna lose," Marty grumbled.

"Whatta you mean, 'we're gonna lose'?" I snapped.

"We weren't gonna beat Kirby. Even with Bobby. But without him we'll get slaughtered," Marty insisted.

"It was stupid what you did, Eddie," Sean chimed in. "We were doing okay and might have scored a few TDs. But you had to blow it over a stupid girl."

"She's not a stupid girl!" I yelled. Then I remembered what I'd said about Mikey liking girls more than football.

"All girls are stupid," Sean replied. "I wish I'd never joined your team. All I did was waste time. Don't call us to practice anymore. We quit."

Then Sean and Marty walked off together, leaving me standing on the corner, the wind whipping through the bare trees and pounding me on all sides.

As I trudged home, I decided that I was a complete loser. When school had started in September, I had a mother and a father who lived in the same house, a football team that played every week, and a best friend. Now I had none of those things. Back then I had never kissed a girl, and now I had, and she was probably too scared to ever speak to me again.

Sixth grade was supposed to be a great year. So far mine was absolutely rotten.

The worst part was what I would have to do the next day: I would have to go to Kirby Carpenter and cancel the game. He would, of course, laugh at me and demand to know why I was canceling. I would never tell him. But he would find out. Like my mom said, bad news travels fast. Pretty soon everybody would know. Then they would let me know that they knew. That's when I'd run away from home. Just like my dad. Run away and leave my problems behind.

When I got home, Mom was making a ton of noise pounding on a chicken with a carving knife and a mallet, and the TV was blaring full-blast. At least we were going to have my favorite, fried chicken, for dinner.

"How was school?" she asked while chopping away at the chicken.

"All right," I mumbled.

"What?!" she asked a bit louder.

"All right!" I shouted.

"Good . . . This darn knife won't cut," she said. Then she started whacking the chicken with a cleaver.

"Turn down the TV, please," I called.

"What?"

"The TV!"

"The TV?"

"Never mind," I said and headed out of the kitchen and up to my room. I tried to forget everything by doing my homework, but the whacking and the TV continued, so I couldn't concentrate at all.

Finally, the whacking and the TV noise stopped. But by the time my mom called me for dinner, my head was pounding like crazy.

I slumped downstairs to the table, where I saw the chicken Mom had been whacking, laid out on a platter, broiled, not fried.

"I thought we were having fried chicken," I whined.

"No. Broiled," my mom replied.

"But you were chopping it up."

"You can eat a broiled chicken whole?"

I flopped into my chair.

"Start," Mom directed me.

Just as I stuck a fork into the smallest piece of chicken on the platter, the phone rang.

"Please don't pick it up," I said.

"I have to. I applied for a job today. It could be them."

But it wasn't them. Just my Aunt Lori. Still, my mom turned away and talked to her about nothing that seemed important. I stared at the piece of chicken on my plate. I tried to nibble at the edges of it, but even the idea of food made me feel sick to my stomach. I decided to leave the chicken alone.

When my mother hung up and turned back to me, she saw I hadn't eaten very much.

"Are you okay?" she asked.

"What do you mean?" I groaned.

"You hardly ate a thing. Did you want fried chicken that bad?"

"I'm not hungry."

"Did you see Bobby today?" my mom asked, lifting a morsel of chicken into her mouth.

"Of course, I saw him. He's in my class."

"I meant, did you talk with him?"

"I wanted to. But he's still mad at me."

"So he's not going to play on Saturday?"

"Nobody's gonna play on Saturday!" I snapped, wondering how she could ask such a stupid question.

"Why not?"

"'Cause you gotta have four players on a team," I told her, my head pounding. "I made the rules. I can't break them."

"You have Marty and Sean. Couldn't you find a fourth?" she asked.

I wanted to tell her that I didn't have Marty and Sean.

That I didn't have Jackie, or Bobby, or anybody, or anything. But right then the phone rang again, and Mom moved to get up from the table.

"No!" I yelled.

"I have to."

"No! No! No!" I screamed, jumping from my chair. Then I picked up my dinner plate, chicken and all, and heaved it across the room. The plate crashed against the wall, exploding into pieces.

"Eddie!"

"Leave me alone!" I cried, bursting into tears.

I rushed from the table, straight to the front door, and out into the windy night.

I ran as fast as I could up my block and turned onto Elwell Road. I tore down Elwell, all the way past school until I reached Washington Street, where I made a left. I ran down Washington, block after block, sucking in as much cold night air as I could until I reached Uncle Joey and Aunt Lori's house. I jumped up the stairs onto their porch and pounded on their door, shivering, and gasping for breath. The porch light came on, and the door opened. Aunt Lori stood there.

"Eddie? What are you doing here?" she asked.

"I need to talk with my dad," I gasped.

"Is everything okay?"

"Yeah. I just need to talk with him."

"He isn't here. He's still at the shop."

Before she even finished the sentence, I was off the porch and rushing up the block. I turned at the corner and headed toward the center of town. I had hardly ever been downtown at night, except a couple of times in the car with my dad, and it always looked kind of creepy. But I had to talk to him. I ran so hard I could barely make sense of where I was, or where I was going. But finally I reached Montgomery Boulevard, the four-lane road that cuts Hartsburg in half. In the distance I saw the big sign that read: PAULSEN'S BODY SHOP. The shop looked dark. But I headed straight for it, like it was the goal line, and I was running back an interception with a minute left to play. Looking in the window, I saw my father working, so I rapped hard on the door.

"What are you doing here?" he asked as he opened the door. He didn't seem too surprised to see me.

"I have to talk to you," I told him.

"Come on in. Where's your coat?"

"I don't have one," I said. I stumbled inside and took a deep breath. The air was warm and smelled of fumes. I began to cough.

"Take it easy, Mister," my dad said.

He got me a cup of water from the cooler, and I swallowed it in two gulps.

"Did you run all the way from home?" he asked.

"I stopped by Uncle Joey's. But Aunt Lori said you weren't there."

"Tonight's my late night. Have to finish up this Corvette. What do you think of her?" he said, pointing to a big, old-looking red car in the bay. "She's a beauty. One of the few reasons I keep working here. Sometimes you see a real beauty."

"Everything's lousy, Dad," I said, trying to get his attention. "I got into a fight with Bobby. The team broke up. We're not gonna play Kirby. And tonight I yelled at Mom. That's why I came over."

"You've got to calm down."

"Nothing's working out right."

"It's hard. I know. But first you've got to get yourself together and calm down," he continued, as if nothing I had said actually mattered.

"Come home," I cried.

"Eddie . . . ," he said, seeming to tense up a little.

"Please come home."

"I can't."

"Why not?"

"I just can't. Someday you'll understand."

"Aunt Lori said men your age get upset if they don't do something big."

"Eddie—"

"I tried to do something big," I interrupted, "and now

everybody hates me. Come home."

"I'm not ready," he said, looking away.

"But we need you."

"Someday you'll understand."

"I understand," I said, really angry. "You don't care about Mom, or me, or anybody. All you care about is yourself."

"That's not true."

"Yes, it is! All you are is selfish!"

I turned and tore out of the shop, back onto Montgomery Boulevard, and then, without thinking, across the boulevard into the traffic. One car screamed to a stop only a few feet away from me, and another blared its horn. But I tore through the traffic and kept on running, all the way up Montgomery to Washington Street, until a pair of headlights lit me up. I turned and recognized the face behind the wheel.

"What are you doing out here so late?" Uncle Joey called from the open window. "Hop in."

I did. And he drove me home.

"I found him on the corner of Montgomery and Washington," Uncle Joey told my mom when he brought me into my house. "I was looking for him when I saw him zip up Montgomery. Boy, can this guy run."

"Thanks, Joey. I really appreciate it," my mother said, trembling.

"No problem at all," Joey said to her. Then he turned to

me and said, "If football doesn't work out, you should try track."

I stood in the living room with my mom without saying a word. I was too scared to move and too scared to talk. I knew she was furious at me. I couldn't even imagine what my punishment would be, but whatever it was, I knew I deserved it.

"Are you okay?" she finally said, but much softer than I thought she would.

I nodded, looking at the ground.

"Look at me, Eddie."

I didn't want to. But I didn't want to disobey her another time. So I turned my head upward just a little. Surprisingly, she didn't look too mad. More concerned than anything else.

"What happened?" she asked me.

"What do you mean?" I whispered.

"At dinner. When you ran out. Why?"

"I was scared."

"Why?"

"I went crazy."

"I know."

I nodded.

"Did you really think running would help?" she went on.

"No," I said, shaking my head.

"Then why did you do it?"

"I didn't think."

"You've got to think," she declared. "You're almost grown."

"Nothing's working out. The team—"

"Don't talk to me about football."

"It's not just football. Everything."

"Sometimes that's how life is. But we've got to stick together, not get angry and run off. I need you, Eddie."

"But I can't do anything right."

"That's not true."

"It is," I insisted.

"No, it isn't, Mister," boomed a big voice from behind me. I turned and saw my father standing in the doorway.

"Trust her," he said. "She's telling you the truth."

Chapter Nine

REMATCH

I stood there as still as I've ever stood in my entire life, almost not believing my eyes. I had yelled at him and run out of the shop only a few minutes before, sure that he would never come home. And there he was, standing in the doorway.

"Dad!" I called out and ran over to him.

"Are you okay?" he asked, hugging me tight.

"Yeah."

"How'd you get home?"

"Uncle Joey picked me up. He was looking for me."

"He shouldn't have had to look for you. It's my fault," he admitted. "I'm sorry for the way I acted at the shop. I was just so surprised to see you . . . No. It was more than that. All I could think of was that dumb Corvette. I was selfish. Just like you said."

"I didn't mean it, Dad."

"You did mean it. And you were right. You came down to the shop at night, which is something you never should do. And I didn't even see it was something important."

"Are you home to stay?" I asked, hoping with all my

strength that he would say yes.

"Are you, Tommy?" Mom asked.

"I didn't want to leave you guys. But I was upset. I didn't know what else to do," Dad said.

"Just so you know, you can't come home tonight and then leave tomorrow," my mom insisted. "If you're coming back, you need to come back for good."

Dad hung his head, looking kind of sad and kind of relieved, and he nodded a little.

My folks sent me to bed pretty soon after that. But I couldn't sleep. Neither could they, because they talked downstairs for hours. I couldn't hear what they were saying through my bedroom door—and I didn't dare try. But every now and then I heard their voices grow stronger, then fade away. Eventually I fell asleep. But when I woke up the next morning, my father was sitting at the kitchen table.

"Good morning," he said.

"Good morning," I smiled nervously. "Are you back for good?"

"Sort of."

"Whatta you mean, 'sort of'?"

"We're going to see how things work out. But I want to be back. You gotta believe me."

Walking to school that morning, I didn't think of football, or Jackie, or anything that might make me upset. I only thought of my dad coming home. And I felt really glad. But I also felt a little nervous, because even though he was home, I couldn't be sure he was going to stay. He had said, "We're going to see how things work out." That meant things might not work out. And if they didn't, he would probably leave again, and probably never come back.

I started thinking about football again when I got to the schoolyard and saw Bobby. Just like yesterday, his face turned hard when we looked at each other.

Then I spotted Jackie in the far corner of the yard with her rope-jumping friends. But today she wasn't jumping. She just stood there, looking totally grim and watching her friends go at it. I wanted to walk over to her, but I was too afraid. If Bobby saw me, he might go crazy again. Even if he didn't hurt me, he would embarrass Jackie. I didn't want that to happen. So I stood by myself until the monitor blew her whistle for us to line up.

When I got home from school, the house was empty. Finally, my mom came home from work and started dinner. She didn't say too much, so I stayed quiet, then headed upstairs to do my homework. Around five-thirty I heard my dad's car pull into the driveway. I rushed downstairs, and in no time the front door opened, and he walked in. He was smiling, but he kept cracking his knuckles like he did when he was nervous. Then he kept walking from room to room, as if he just couldn't get comfortable.

When we sat down to eat, he must have noticed I was tense, too, because he asked, "What's the matter, Mister? You're pretty quiet tonight."

"I guess," I mumbled.

"If there's something wrong, tell me about it," he said.

I wanted to tell him there were a lot of things wrong—and that he was one of them. But I decided to stay clear of that. Instead, I focused on the other main thing wrong in my life: Bobby.

"I wanna talk to him," I said. "But he seems so angry."

"He really went crazy on you?" Dad asked.

"Totally."

"Your mother told me you were kissing his sister."

"Yeah," I admitted.

"I can see where he might not like that. But to get violent. There's no excuse."

I nodded in agreement.

"I guess you're not gonna play football on Saturday?"

"Nope," I said, shaking my head.

"Still, you're best friends. You've got to get back with him somehow, football game or no football game."

Yeah. I had to get back with Bobby. But I had no idea how.

When dinner ended, Dad threw out the garbage and went inside to watch the news while Mom and I did the dishes.

While I was drying the dishes, I began to feel really tired. After we'd finished, I told Mom I was going upstairs to lie down. But when I got to the staircase, the sports report was on. I heard a voice from the TV say, "And now an interview with Jets coach Herman Edwards."

I quickly stuck my head in the living room.

"Well, Coach. The Jets have lost four in a row. What are your plans for this Sunday?" the reporter asked.

"I'm making a change," the coach answered. "We're starting Chad Pennington this week. Maybe I was too quick to switch to a new system. After all, the old one had its weaknesses, but overall it worked pretty well. I'm gonna see if it can get us a win."

Then it all made sense. I knew what I had to do. And I was going to start right away.

First I called Mikey.

"Get the team back together?" he asked, sounding totally surprised.

"Yeah," I replied.

"And play Kirby Carpenter on Saturday?"

"Yeah."

"But you're the one who broke the team up."

"I know. And I was wrong," I admitted. "Now I'm trying to make it right. Whatta you say?"

"I don't know, Eddie. Did you call Kenny yet?"

"No."

"Call Kenny. If he says yes, then I'll say yes, too."

I knew Kenny would be harder. That's why I called Mikey first. I had no choice, so I gave Kenny a call.

"Get the team back together?!" he squealed after I told him my plan.

"Yeah," I replied.

"No way!" he cried. "You broke it up. Now you want me back just to get slaughtered by Kirby Carpenter on Saturday."

"We're not gonna get slaughtered."

"We always get slaughtered," he went on, "'cause you call lousy plays."

"Kenny—"

"And why should I play with Bobby? He's always staring at me, telling me I better not call him and hang up anymore. I never called him and hung up in my life."

"I believe you, Kenny," I tried.

"I believe you're a jerk."

"Kenny—"

"And I'm hanging up on you."

Then, without thinking, I tried my last play.

"Don't you ever wanna beat Kirby?"

"Sure, I wanna beat Kirby."

"Have you?"

"Huh?"

"Have you beat him since we broke up?"

"You know I haven't," he said, his voice weakening.

"Have you played him?"

"No."

"Have you played any game, with anybody, anywhere?"

"No," he said, sounding really disappointed. "And it's all your fault."

"It is. That's why I wanna get us back together. To make it right. Even if it's just for one game."

"I don't know," Kenny said, starting to break.

"Come on, Kenny," I continued. "It was my fault. Now I'm trying to apologize. Just one more game."

The next morning we met in the schoolyard. Kenny and Mikey were looking pretty angry when I got there. But after I told them we had some new plays and really had a chance to beat Kirby, their cold expressions turned warmer. Finally they smiled, and I knew I had them. Then I told them about Bobby.

"He what?!" Kenny yelled.

"He kinda left the team," I explained. "But I have a plan to get him back."

After school we headed to my house, picked up my cut-up, dirty, old football, and then went over to practice as loud as possible in front of Bobby's house. We hoped his love to play football would force him to come outside.

First we started with down-and-outs.

"Kenny!" I yelled and threw him the ball.

"Yeah!" Kenny yelled back, catching it.

"Mikey!" I yelled and heaved it toward him.

He grabbed it, tucked it in, and called out "Yeah!"

Then we went to down-and-ins.

When we switched to post patterns, I saw a curtain move in Jackie's window. A few seconds later Jackie looked out at me. She waved, big enough for me and only me to see. I waved back. Not big, but big enough for her to see. I knew if Bobby was watching that this might set him off again. But I didn't care. I wasn't going to sacrifice Jackie for a team, no matter how much I wanted to get the team back together.

Then I taught Kenny and Mikey a few of my new plays. When we got to the double hook slant, the front door blew open, and Bobby stomped out onto his front steps.

"What are you doing in front of my house?!" he demanded.

"We're practicing for tomorrow's game," I called back.

"I'm not talking to you, Eddie!" he shouted. He then looked at Mikey and called out the same question.

"We're practicing for tomorrow's game," Mikey replied. "And we want you to practice with us."

"I would never practice with you. Never in a million years. Never with Kenny. And never ever with Eddie."

"Then why are you out on your steps?" Mikey asked.

"'Cause I want you to go away."

I decided to jump back in.

"We're never gonna go away," I called out. "You know why? 'Cause we like you. And we wanna play with you."

"If you liked me, you wouldn't have kissed my sister," Bobby shouted, sounding madder.

"I like you, Bobby. You're my best friend. But I like Jackie, too."

"No way!"

"I'm sorry for what I did. And I'm even sorrier for making you mad. But I like her. And nothing you ever say or do is gonna stop me from liking her."

"I don't want you kissing my sister. Or talking to her. Or liking her. Or even thinking about her."

"Then beat me up now. Kenny and Mikey won't stop you. Come down here and beat me up. 'Cause I'm gonna talk to Jackie."

"Go home!"

"You think I'm gonna get her to like me, then go away, and make her upset. But I'm not going away. So either beat me up now, or come play with us," I insisted. "You're still my best friend."

Bobby stood there for a long moment. Then he spun around, stomped inside, and slammed the door behind him. My muscles immediately went limp, and my head began to droop.

But then the door was thrown open again, and Bobby stomped back onto the steps.

"Did you mean what you said?" he cried.

"Yeah."

"That you won't go away?"

"Yeah."

"That you want me to play with you?"

"Yeah."

"That I'm still your friend?"

I felt a smile begin to break across my face, and called out a very loud, "Yeah!"

"Then I'll play with you," Bobby said. He jumped down his front steps and ran into the street. "But Kenny's got to promise to stop prank calling my house."

I shot Kenny a look that said "just do it," and he shrugged and said, "Okay. Whatever."

"Let's play!" announced Bobby.

The next morning was cold and bright. I figured it was probably the last sunny day before everything turned December gray. I shivered when I got out of bed and wasn't sure if it was from the weather or all that was happening. But when I went down to the kitchen for breakfast and saw Dad scrambling some eggs, I felt better—and really hungry.

"All ready?" he asked with a smile.

"Pretty much," I told him.

After finishing breakfast I went back upstairs to brush my teeth, put on my game clothes, and get my football. When I came down, my folks were waiting for me.

"Be careful," my mom said.

"Play tough," my dad said. "And good luck."

"I'm gonna need it," I admitted.

"You're going to play with your old ball?" my dad asked.

I looked down at my football, nicked and cut and covered with mud splatters from all my games since I'd been playing.

"Yeah, Dad," I said, my throat getting tight.

"What about your new ball?"

"I think I should play with this one."

He thought for a moment, then said, "I understand."

My team practiced in the park for an hour before Kirby and his Giants showed up.

"What's going on?" Kirby bellowed when he saw Kenny and Mikey.

"You said you'd play any team I wanted. Even the real Jets. Well, these are my Jets," I shot back at him.

"We're gonna kill you," he said, sneering at us. "Call it in the air.

So he flipped a coin. Kirby won, and we threw off to him.

As soon as Kirby's Giants got the ball, they marched right down the field. Four passes and they scored. Obviously, our defense was a little rusty.

Then we got the ball. On the first play, I threw a quick-out to Bobby for a short gain. But on second and third downs, Kenny and Mikey dropped their passes, so we had to punt.

On the second series, the third series, and the fourth series, Kirby's team scored. Not only did they score, but they scored easily. A screen over the middle, with none of us covering. Then a bomb down the right sideline, over Kenny's head and into Sammy Green's hands. Finally, a modified flea flicker, just like mine. But theirs worked, while mine had been a bust. It was a rout. Kirby and his teammates were laughing at us like we were clowns in the circus.

After we were stopped on our fifth series, Kirby got the ball and marched down the field again. One more touchdown and they would win—and we would be more embarrassed than we had ever been.

Kirby walked up to the line, the sneer of all sneers across his face, and yelled "Hike!"

I flipped him the ball and started counting "Mississippis" while jumping up and down as high as I could.

He took three giant steps backwards, then hurled a bomb just like before, right toward Sammy Green. But this time

Kenny jumped up in front of Sammy and pulled the ball down with such force that his glasses flew off his nose.

"Yes!" I yelled, as we all rushed over to pile on top of Kenny.

"Come on. Let's play ball," Kirby grumbled while we were still celebrating.

"Now we're playing," I told my teammates.

And we were. We started moving right away. Old plays. New plays. Things I made up as we moved downfield.

Then I threw a long down-and-out in the dirt to Bobby for a touchdown.

"Yes!" I yelled, when he hit the ground, the ball gripped tightly in his hands.

"Wow," Bobby said, looking back at me with a face full of dirt.

When Kirby got the ball back, he went nowhere.

We got the ball. I threw two passes to Kenny, two to Mikey, and finished it off with my double hook slant to Bobby for another touchdown.

We scored on our next series, and the series after that. For the first time in the history of the Juniper Street Jets, we were tied with Kirby Carpenter's Giants.

Kirby got the ball again, but threw three incomplete passes, then angrily kicked the ball about twenty feet away, and screamed at his teammates. I beamed because everything was finally coming together.

Kirby punted to us, and we headed straight up the field. Mikey pulled in a short pass with his huge hands. Then Kenny took one straight in his skinny gut. I was putting more zip on the ball than I ever had.

Then I got the team into a huddle and announced the play: "The fade-out, fade-in bomb."

"No, no, no," Kenny whined.

"Why not?"

"They're expecting it," he replied.

"I haven't called it once today. They'll be completely surprised."

"I don't know, Eddie. Kenny's got a point," Mikey said.

"You've never liked that play. Neither of you. But now's the time," I insisted. I turned to Bobby and asked, "Are you ready?"

"You bet," he declared.

We broke the huddle and headed up to the line, one pass away from victory.

I looked over at Kirby. His teeth were gritted so tight that he looked like he might need a crowbar to pry them apart.

"Hike!" I yelled, and dropped straight back.

First I looked right to Mikey.

Then I looked left to Kenny. But he wasn't my main target.

In the corner of my eye I saw Bobby start to fade in to the middle of the field.

I pulled the ball way back and threw it as long and as hard as I possibly could. It flew straight through the cold breeze, high against the icy blue background, until it finally began to fall. As it fell, I began to taste our victory. Like steaming-hot spaghetti and meatballs, it tasted great. But as Bobby stuck out his hand to grab the ball, Kirby Carpenter appeared out of nowhere, leaped into the air, and stole it away.

"No!" I yelled.

But it was already too late. Kirby whipped up the field, past Mikey, and past Kenny, who had both been caught flat-footed. I tried to move to my left as fast as possible, but Kirby was moving like an Indy car.

In desperation I lunged at him, my arms so far outstretched they felt like they were going to pop out of their sockets. But I wasn't even close. I fell to the ground, getting nothing but a face full of dirt.

"Yes!" Kirby screamed, spiking the ball into the dirt. "Yes!"

My teammates and I stood there, feeling like the lowest lifeforms in the universe, while Kirby and his Giants howled over their victory. Finally, Kirby turned and walked toward me. I was sure he was gonna say something mean, just liked he always did. But he broke into a broad smile, and said, "We won. But you guys played pretty good. See ya next week." Then he and his teammates all walked away, until the only sound in the park was the whistling of the winter wind.

I knew I had to say something. I didn't want to. What I wanted to do was die, then decompose, then disappear. But since I knew that wasn't going to happen, I just said, "Sorry, guys."

"It's okay," Kenny said, not seeming mad at me at all.

"Yeah. Things happen," Mikey agreed.

"We played really good," Bobby said. "We just hafta keep playing."

We agreed to practice again on Monday and then headed out of the park. When Kenny and Mikey turned toward Arlington Street, I called, "See you Monday!"

"See you!" they called back.

Bobby and I walked up Boswell Road. Neither of us spoke for several blocks. Finally Bobby said, "I'm sorry about what happened."

"We shoulda won. I didn't see Kirby in time—"

"Not about the game," Bobby continued. "About Jackie. And what I did." His face was filled with sadness. "I just got so crazy. My mom got really mad at me. She grounded me for a month. Today's game was the only thing she said I could do."

"Wow," I said.

"Yeah. Wow."

"I want us to stay friends."

"Me, too."

When we reached Eldridge Street, we stopped and turned toward each other.

"See you Monday," Bobby said.

"I'll call you tonight," I replied.

"Good idea," he said.

"And about Jackie," I attempted. "I really do like her."

"I know," Bobby replied.

As I headed home, I kicked at the ground more than a few times over losing the game. We really could have won this one. But I blew it, calling the wrong play at the wrong time. Bad timing seemed to be one of my big problems. I knew it was something I had to work on. Still, as I continued walking home, the disappointment began to fade, and I started to feel better—not because we had played well, but because we had played at all. A day earlier getting the team together seemed nearly impossible. But we did come together. We all made it happen.

But what made me feel happiest was having my family back together again. Although my dad had only been back two nights, and I knew he still wasn't the happiest person in the world, I had a good feeling that he was back to stay.

When I turned onto Juniper Street, I saw him in the driveway. He was bundled up in a heavy jacket, a bright green Jets cap on his head, working on his car. He turned around, looked straight at me, and shot me his big smile. I smiled back at him, pulled my football way back, and threw it high into the air.

Attanas, John   45456

JATT

Eddie and the Jets

DATE DUE		
JUL 22 2011		